THE BILLIONAIRE
WHO SAW
HER BEAUTY

THE BILLIONAIRE WHO SAW HER BEAUTY

BY

REBECCA WINTERS

MILLS & BOON

First published in Great Britain 2016
By Mills & Boon, an imprint of HarperCollins*Publishers*
1 London Bridge Street, London, SE1 9GF

Large Print edition 2016

ISBN: 978-0-263-26235-3

Our policy is to use papers that are natural, renewable and recyclable products and made from wood grown in sustainable forests. The logging and manufacturing processes conform to the legal environmental regulations of the country of origin.

Printed and bound in Great Britain
by CPI Antony Rowe, Chippenham, Wiltshire

This is for my super-marvellous father,
Dr John Z. Brown, Jr, who was adored
by his many thousands of patients during
his long career. I've praised him before
in other books because he was the best!

CHAPTER ONE

"SIGNOR MONTANARI?"

Rini was just getting in the limo. He looked around in the direction of one of the reporters who'd followed him outside the doors of the fourteenth-century Palazzo Colonna in Rome. Dozens of them had assembled to cover the European Congress of Businessmen.

"A moment of your time, *per favore*—one piece of news I can use for my lead story in *La Repubblica*?"

Why not?

"Since Italy imports almost all of its hydrocarbon demand, a doubling of domestic production would help the country reduce its energy bill. I'm planning to find them in Italy."

"Where?"

"That's my secret for now."

The reporter beamed for having been given a partial scoop. "*Mille grazie, signor.*"

He nodded and closed the door before his driver took him to the heliport for the flight to his mountaintop villa in Positano, on the Amalfi Coast. Now that the two-day September conference covering the economic problems facing Europe was over, Rini was eager to explore his latest project. On Monday he'd be leaving for the coast of Southern Italy, but tonight he had other plans.

Once the helicopter landed on the pad behind his villa, he jumped down and found his housekeeper, Bianca, out by the pool watering the tubs of flowers. She looked up when she saw him.

"Welcome back."

"It's good to be home."

"How's your father?"

"Well as can be expected." Rini had flown to Naples after yesterday's session and spent the night with his *papà*, who seemed to be handling the loss of Rini's mother a little better these days. She'd been the heart of their home and Rini would always miss her happy, optimistic spirit.

"Was the conference beneficial?"

"I'm not sure *beneficial* is the right word. *Chilling* would be more accurate. Europe is in trouble economically, but I'd rather not think about that tonight."

"Do you want dinner?"

"I'd love one of your meals, but I'm meeting Guido tonight. It's his birthday." His best friend from childhood, the son of Leonides Rossano, who owned Rossano shipping lines, had texted him earlier in the day:

The parents are throwing a party for me on the yacht. Please say you can make it. I know you're at a conference, but I need your advice about something serious. By the time you arrive it will be breaking up so we can talk in private.

The message sounded serious, even for Guido, who clearly wasn't in a celebratory mood. He obviously had no plans for the weekend with a woman. His friend was as bad as Rini, who had no plans in that department, either. The two of them made quite a pair, but for entirely different reasons.

Guido was still looking for the right woman who hadn't come along yet. Rini didn't have the same problem. The right woman wasn't out there for him because she wouldn't want him when he had to tell her he was infertile. An old soccer injury he'd suffered in his youth had made it impossible for him to give any woman a child.

The pain of that realization had grown worse with every passing year, increasing his dissatisfaction with his own personal life. Whenever he did meet a woman he cared about, he held back, not allowing the relationship to develop into something deeper. It always came down to his fear she would reject him if she knew the truth.

He'd been denying his deep-seated needs for such a long time, he'd forgotten what real fulfillment was like. Since his sister Valentina—the mother of two children and now ecstatically married—had recently moved out of his villa, his unhappiness had deepened.

She'd lived with him through her whole pregnancy. He'd helped her with the baby when she'd first come home from the hospital. He'd loved every minute of it, but he'd carried a secret pain in his heart because he knew *he'd* never be able to be a birth father. When she'd married Giovanni and moved out, Rini felt the emptiness of the villa. It echoed the emptiness in his soul for what could never be.

Valentina's happiness, not to mention that of his younger brother, Carlo, who enjoyed a wonderful marriage and had a little girl, heightened his awareness that the key element in his life was missing. He envied his brother for being able to give his wife a child. Rini's doctor had told him he was a fool to let that prevent him from falling in love. "The right woman will be able to handle it," he'd reminded him.

Rini didn't believe it as he walked through the villa to his suite and stripped for a shower to get ready. After slipping into his black tuxedo, he reached for the wrapped gift he'd bought for the occasion. Once he'd said goodbye to Bianca, he left for the helicopter. The new hand-tied fishing fly he'd purchased for Guido was reputed to bring results. They often fished the mountain streams for trout. He thought his friend would be pleased.

Twenty minutes later he landed on board the Rossano luxury superyacht moored in the Bay of Naples, reminding him that not everyone was feeling the economic crunch. The yacht boasted seventeen staterooms and all the amenities of a five-star hotel, including a swimming pool and dance floor.

Twilight had descended, lending magic to the

spectacular surroundings of one of the most beautiful and photographed bays in the world, with Mount Vesuvius in the background. He told his pilot to come back later and jumped down as Guido strode over to him.

"I've been waiting for you. Saw you on the evening news. Impressive stuff. I was afraid you wouldn't be able to make it. Thanks for coming."

"As if I'd miss your birthday." He pulled the small package out of his jacket and handed it to him. *"Buon compleanno."*

They gave each other a hug, then walked into the salon-cum-bar for a drink. He opened his present and held up the lure. "Just what I need."

"Good. Let's go fishing next weekend. I'll clear my schedule for next Saturday." Rini had been working himself into the ground and needed a break.

"Perfect." With a smile of satisfaction he put the present in his pocket. With dark blond hair, good-looking Guido could have his pick of any woman. The money behind his family name made him sought after and somewhat cynical, as he feared no woman saw him for himself. Guido was the best friend Rini could ever have had. He hoped the only son of Leonides Rossano would end up one day with a woman worthy enough to win his heart.

Rini's name and wealth made him a target, too. Women came on to him, causing him to question if any of them loved him for himself. Coupled with his problem of infertility, Rini imagined it was possible he'd end up a bachelor for good.

"Was it a nice party?"

"Different. One of the big fashion houses asked Father for permission to film a show on the yacht. You missed the whole thing."

"Sorry about that. The meeting in Rome went longer than anticipated."

Rini followed him down the steps to the deck, where he greeted his friend's parents and family, who made up some of Naples's most elite socialites and were beautifully dressed. Rini was well acquainted with many of them. An orchestra played music and the drinks were flowing.

They moved over to the area where a smorgasbord had been set up. By now he was hungry. After filling his plate, he joined his friend at one of the tables away from the others, where they could eat and talk alone.

"Your text said you wanted advice. What's going on with you?"

Guido started to say something when his father broke in on them. Two attractive women with long hair he hadn't seen before were with him. Rini exchanged a glance with his friend, who looked annoyed at the interruption. They both got to their feet.

"Dea Loti and Daphne Butelli, may I present my son Guido and his best friend, Rinieri Montanari."

"How do you do," Rini said, eyeing both of them.

"You missed their show, Rini," the older man interjected.

"As I indicated earlier, I was unavoidably detained on business."

"Well, you're here now. They have to leave on the tender in a few minutes. Maybe you could give them a dance before they go?"

Guido's father never stopped hoping his son would meet the woman he couldn't live without. Rini knew his friend was upset at being railroaded, but agreed to the request. "It would be our pleasure."

He gravitated toward the woman closest to him, who was dressed in purple. After walking her over to the dance floor, he drew her in his arms. "I've never been to a fashion show before. I'm sorry I missed it."

"I doubt it's the kind of thing the CEO of Montanari's generally does on the weekend." By now Guido was dancing with the other model.

"I understand it's hard work. Did you have a chance to eat yet? We don't have to dance if you're hungry."

"Thank you, but no. I don't want anything. I have to watch my figure."

"Well, your discipline definitely shows."

She flashed him a beguiling smile. "Do you live in Naples?"

"No, but I work here."

It surprised him when her hands slid up his chest and around his neck. "Daphne and I are going to be in Naples one more night because of an afternoon show at the Grand Hotel Parker's, then we have another show in Rome. Perhaps we could get together tomorrow evening for dinner after the show?"

Her eyes stared up at him in unmistakable invitation.

"I'm afraid my plans are indefinite at the moment, but I've certainly enjoyed this dance with you."

She held her smile. "Well, if you straighten them out, call me around seven at the Grand Hotel Vesuvio, where I'm staying, and ask for Signorina Loti." In the next breath she planted a hungry kiss on his lips he hadn't been prepared for. Then she darted away.

Rini went back to the table to wait for Guido. In a few minutes his friend joined him. "Sorry my father did that to us." One eyebrow lifted. "After the kiss she gave you just now, are you going to see her again?"

"No." Her pushy style had put him off. "What about you?"

"Not interested. You know damn well Papà told her you're the most eligible bachelor in Italy, next to me, of course." He said it without mirth.

Rini shook his head.

Guido studied him. "Maybe she decided to try the direct approach to get beneath your armor."

"I'm afraid it didn't work."

An exasperated sigh escaped. "Papà doesn't know when to give up. In fact it's because of him I need to talk to you. I've made a decision to take a year off from the family business to invest in something I really want to do. He won't like it, but I want your opinion. Come on. Let's get a drink in the bar."

Rini followed him, wondering what was on his friend's mind.

After a dive with colleagues that produced no new finds, twenty-eight-year-old Alessandra Caracciolo returned home late Monday afternoon. Bruno Tozzi had left his scuba gear in the cruiser with hers and would come by for it in a day or two. Instinct told her he'd done it on purpose so he'd have an excuse to see her again.

Since their last dive, when Bruno had buddied her, he'd made it no secret that he wanted to be with her all the time, but she didn't have romantic feelings for him. Though she dove with him and their friends for their work, that had to be the extent of their relationship. The next time they were together, she would make it clear she wasn't interested and never could be.

She tied the boat to the dock of her family's private pier. Garbed in flip-flops and a man's long-sleeved shirt that she'd thrown over her blue-and-white polka-dotted bikini, she headed for the Land Rover with her duffel bag.

Once in the car, she drove on sand past the helipad and around to the front of the castle. When she reached it, she would take a shower and wash her hair. Alessandra wore it neck-length because she spent so much time in the water. It dried fast and the natural curl made it easy to take care of.

As she pulled up near the main entrance, she saw a limo parked in the courtyard, making her curious. All vehicles came across the causeway from the mainland at Metaponto, a port town of Basilicata, Italy. But after five o'clock, any visitors were escorted out by staff.

Their family's castle on the tiny island of Posso off the Ionian coast dated back to Queen Joanna of Naples, who ruled in 1343. Besides tourists from Bari and Taranto, who were al-lowed visits to the castle four hours a day on Tuesdays and Wednesdays with a guide, dignitaries from the world over called on her father, Count Onorato Caracciolo, asking favors because of his influence in the region.

Alessandra got out of the car and hurried inside past the tapestry of the queen hanging on the wall in the huge front foyer. She headed for the grand staircase, eager to make herself scarce until she'd cleaned up.

The moment she reached the first step, a deep male voice called to her. *"Signorina?"*

She whirled around to see a tall, incredibly gorgeous dark-haired man in a charcoal-colored business suit walking toward her, his dark brows furrowed. Still holding the duffel bag in one hand, Alessandra clutched the railing with the other.

He stared at her so strangely. "I thought I was hallucinating, but it *is* you. Since Saturday night you've cut your hair. I don't understand. How did you know I was coming here today? On the yacht you told me you had another show to do in Rome," he murmured.

The way his piercing black-brown eyes played over her face and figure, she knew he had a history with her identical twin, Dea. He was the most striking male Alessandra had ever seen in her life. She found herself envying her beautiful sister for having met him first and couldn't fault her taste. Men had never been able to resist her.

Alessandra cleared her throat. "I'm sorry, *signor*, but I'm not Dea."

Embarrassed to be caught looking so messy and disheveled after her diving trip, she ran up the steps without looking back. Her sister would never allow herself to be seen like this. All the way to the next floor she felt the man's penetrating eyes on her retreating back and bare legs, causing her to tremble.

Had her sister finally met the one she'd been looking for? Dea had always kept their family identity private. Because she was a model, she called herself Dea Loti so no one would know she was the daughter of Count Caracciolo. For her to divulge her secret to this man meant their relationship must have turned serious, otherwise he wouldn't have known where she lived.

No doubt she'd invited him to come. Did she want the family to meet him? But his scrutiny of Alessandra led her to believe he hadn't looked pleased to see her here. Maybe Dea hadn't told him she had a twin. Alessandra didn't know what to think.

If only she hadn't arrived back from her dive trip until tomorrow, this wouldn't have happened and she wouldn't be haunted by that man's image engraved on her mind. It shocked her to realize that at long last there might be an important man in her sister's life. Alessandra knew her sister's quest had been to find the perfect man while she made the most of her modeling career. Their parents would be overjoyed.

Six years ago she and Dea had gone through a terrible experience involving a man, one Alessandra had hoped to marry. But when he met Dea, he fell for her and followed her to Rome. Their relationship didn't last, but the pain of betrayal had cut Alessandra like a knife and it had taken a long time to recover. Since the falling out with her sister, no man of importance had come into either of their lives.

In the last two years she'd tried to put the past behind her and get back the friendship they'd once shared. Dea came and went from home according to her hectic schedule and their family had enjoyed some good times. Evidently this past summer Dea had found romance after she'd gone back to Rome. Love on a yacht, no less... If that gorgeous man owned it, then he could keep her in the lifestyle she desired.

But for some reason Alessandra had been oddly upset by the encounter in the foyer, unable to understand why. *Except that she really could...* These days her own love life was nonexistent.

Once inside the bedroom, Alessandra plopped the duffel bag on the floor and got out of her clothes. Her mind was still on Dea, whom she hadn't seen for six weeks. Her sister had developed an interest in fashion and modeling at an early age and that hadn't changed.

Alessandra led a different life altogether. She couldn't remember when she didn't have an interest in the archaeology of this region of Italy. The island castle itself was built on an ancient archaeological site. Since college she'd been involved in several multidisciplinary studies in the field of archaeology within a Mediterranean perspective, with particular emphasis on Southern Italy.

Without being able to scuba dive, she could never have achieved her dream to do the necessary underwater work with friends she'd made among the archaeological staff at the University of Catania. Scuba diving wasn't for everyone. Dea couldn't understand her passion for it, but it didn't matter because their parents approved and supported both her and Dea in their individual endeavors.

After a shower and shampoo, she blow-dried her hair, then dressed in pleated tan pants and an ivory-colored linen blouse. With an application of coral frost lipstick, she left the room on khaki wedgies and went in search of her parents. They'd married for love and were very close. Unlike many couples, they did everything together whether it was for business or pleasure. Though Alessandra had never discussed it with Dea, their parents' happy marriage had been the ultimate role model for both sisters.

On the way to their apartment she saw Liona, the wiry housekeeper who'd come to work for them at eighteen and had been with them ever since. She was like another member of the family and ran the large staff with precision.

"If you're looking for your *mamma,* she left for Taranto two days ago to help your aunt, who fell and broke her hip."

"Oh, no! Poor Fulvia."

"She'll be all right, but your mother will probably be gone for a few more days."

"I need to call them."

They started down the staircase together.

"I'm glad you're back. You know how your father worries."

Liona was the one who worried about Alessandra. She thought scuba diving was dangerous. Alessandra gave her a hug. "It's good to see you. How's Alfredo?" Liona's cat had been sick.

"The vet says he's getting old and shouldn't go up and down stairs."

"I'll help carry him for you."

"Bless you. Did you have any luck on this last diving trip?"

"I wish."

"Oh, well. Another time. Are you hungry? I'll tell the cook."

"Please don't bother her. I'll find something to eat later. Thanks, Liona."

She hurried toward her father's office, wondering if the male visitor was still with him, then scoffed with impatience because the man was on her mind at all.

"Ciao, Papà."

"Alessandra!" Her grayish blond father stood

up from his desk and hugged her. "You were gone too long this time."

"It was only a week."

"We always miss you. Did you have a good time?"

"Yes, even if we didn't find anything of significance." She walked around to sit in one of the leather chairs facing his desk. "I'd much rather know about you and mom. Liona told me Zia Fulvia broke her hip and Mom went to Taranto to help her."

He nodded. "Your aunt will make a full recovery. Your mother could be back tomorrow."

"Oh, good. So tell me what else has been happening while I've been away."

His brows lifted. "Something unexpected. I'm glad you're back so we can talk. More than anyone else I want your input because you have a fine mind."

"I got it from you and Mamma." Her comment produced a chuckle. So maybe her assumption had been right. "It wouldn't have anything to do with the man I saw in the foyer earlier this evening, would it?"

He cocked his head. "Actually it would. When did you see him?"

"I'd just come in the castle when he spoke to me."

"Did he introduce himself to you?"

"No. It wasn't like that. On my way up the staircase he mistook me for Dea before he headed for your office, that's all."

Her father nodded. "I guess I shouldn't be surprised. Her face is everywhere."

"Papà—" She smiled at him. "Are you pretending with me?"

"About what?"

"Was he here because of her?"

The count blinked. "Not that I know of."

"Oh." She needed to keep her thoughts to herself. "Who is he?"

He smiled. "If you didn't live in your world of books and ancient underwater artifacts, you would have recognized him as the CEO of

Italy's most powerful engineering dynasty, Rinieri Montanari."

She stirred in the chair. "Of course I recognize the Montanari name. Who wouldn't?" It explained the man's aura of authority.

Her father sat back and touched the tips of his fingers together. "His family has accumulated great wealth. He's the brilliant one driving the company to new heights. A week ago he made an appointment to come and see me about a business proposition."

"That sounds interesting."

"I'll give you a little background. Night before last he was on the news following the European Congress of Businessmen held in Rome. I saw the gleam in his eyes. He said he had secret plans to grow the economy. Today we talked and arranged for him to come back tomorrow to get into the details."

He'd aroused her curiosity. "What is he after?"

"He'd like to drill for oil on our property."

Alessandra shifted in the chair. "He and doz-

ens of others who've wanted the same thing for
the last half century," she muttered. "Since he
knows it's not for sale, why is he coming back?"

"This man is different from all the others. He
wants to lease the land."

Lease? "Are you considering letting him?"

"I'm thinking about it."

"Wow."

Her father eyed her curiously. "Why do you
say that?"

"I thought our property was inviolate."

"Leasing isn't the same thing as selling."

"You're right."

"Alessandra, something's on your mind. Why
did you ask if he was here because of Dea? Has
your sister confided in you about him?"

"No, Papà. In fact I haven't spoken to her for
almost two months."

"Hmm. If he'd met her before, he didn't mention anything about meeting her to me."

"Why would he if he didn't know anything
about our family?"

"But what if he does know? It makes me wonder what came first, the chicken or the egg?"

"What do you mean?"

"He might have met Dea before he ever called me."

Alessandra was trying to understand what her father was getting at. "Why is this troubling you so much?"

"I'm your loving *papà*. My daughters were born princesses of the Houses of Taranto and Caracciolo. Because of our family history, you know I've always wanted to protect you from unscrupulous men."

His explanation surprised her. "That sounds like medieval thinking. Papà, you don't honestly think the CEO of Montanari Engineering fits in that category?" *That gorgeous man? The one she'd envied Dea for meeting first?* Alessandra didn't want to believe it. Something about him had impressed her deeply.

"Though we don't use the titles anymore, there are some men who try to calculate the monetary worth of our family. There's nothing they would like more than to acquire your bank accounts and assets more than your love."

Alessandra frowned. "The man comes from his own family dynasty and doesn't need more."

"One would assume as much, but for some men one dynasty isn't enough." His gaze swerved to hers. "I don't want to think it. But if he has targeted Dea to marry her and eventually gain possession of our property, I don't like the thought of it."

She didn't like it, either. Not at all. "Personally I don't believe it." Alessandra didn't want to believe it. Not about that man. Whatever history her sister and Signor Montanari might have together, she didn't want to think about it. To be with a man like him...

Alessandra got to her feet. "Don't let it bother you, Papà. Have you had dinner yet?"

"No."

"I'll bring you something."

"*Grazie*, but I'm not hungry."

"I'm afraid I am. I haven't eaten since I got back. Excuse me while I grab a sandwich. If you want me, I'll be in the library."

Alessandra left the office and headed for the kitchen to find something to eat. Afterward she walked to the castle library on the main floor, the repository of their family history where she could be alone. Years earlier she'd turned one corner of it into her own office, complete with file cabinets and a state-of-the-art computer and printer, plus a large-screen television for viewing the many videos she'd compiled. This had been her inner sanctum for years.

She sat down at the desk and got back to work on the book she was writing about Queen Joanna. Just as she'd settled down to get busy, the phone rang. It was her father.

"Papà?"

"I just wanted to let you know I've got business in Metaponto. The pilot is flying me in a few minutes."

"Do you want company? I'll go with you."

"Not tonight, *piccola*." Her father's endearment for her. When Alessandra was born, she was the younger twin by three minutes and the name *little one* stuck. "I'm sure you're tired after your scuba-diving trip, so you get some sleep and we'll talk in the morning. I could be gone a couple of hours and will probably get back late tonight."

"All right."

While she got back to work she heard her father's helicopter fly away. She kept busy for another hour, then went upstairs to get ready for bed. But when she slid under the covers, she didn't fall asleep right away. Memories of the past with her sister filtered through her mind.

Though their personalities were entirely different, she and Dea had been as close as any two sisters until college, when Francesco had come into Alessandra's life. She'd fallen in love and they talked about getting married. But before they got engaged he met Dea, who was more confident than Alessandra and had already started her modeling career.

Her sister had a beauty and lovability that had drawn guys to her from her teens. By contrast, Alessandra felt rather dull and unexciting. Certainly she wasn't as attractive. But she'd always accepted those truths and never let them affect their friendship. Not until Francesco had laid eyes on Dea. From that moment everything changed. Alessandra felt herself lose him and there wasn't anything she could do about it.

He followed her sister to Rome and she never saw him again. Francesco sent Alessandra a letter explaining he couldn't help falling in love with Dea and hoped she wouldn't hate him too badly. As for Dea, Alessandra didn't see her for two months. When her sister came home, she told Alessandra she was sorry for what had happened. She explained that Francesco had done all the running, and she'd soon found out he was a loser. Alessandra was lucky to be out of the relationship.

The trauma of being betrayed by Francesco and her sister had completely floored her. It had taken a long time to work past the pain. Though they'd shared sisterly love in the past, from that time on they'd had a troubled relationship and two truths emerged. Alessandra didn't know if she could trust a man again and Dea would always be the beautiful one who usually got the best of Alessandra. People seemed to love her the most.

Alessandra had to live with the knowledge that she was known as the clever one, a scholar with a sense of adventure. She'd thought that by the age of twenty-eight she would have finally gotten past her jealousy of Dea's ability to attract men. But it wasn't true. Otherwise meeting Signor Montanari, who'd met Dea first, wouldn't have disturbed Alessandra so much.

If her father was right, what a sad irony that this man might be using Dea to get what he really wanted, making both sisters appear as poor judges of character. First the chef Alessandra had fallen for who couldn't remain faithful once he'd laid eyes on Dea. Now Signor Montanari, who looked like the embodiment of a woman's dreams. But what if her father learned this man had a secret agenda? The troubling thought kept her tossing and turning all night.

CHAPTER TWO

ON TUESDAY MORNING Alessandra awakened and headed to the bathroom for a quick shower. She dressed in jeans and a blouse. After brushing her hair and applying lipstick, she walked down the hall past the stairs to her parents' apartment wearing her sandals.

She knocked on the door with no result, so she opened it and called out, "Papà?" He was probably in the sitting room drinking coffee while he read his newspapers, but the room was empty. Frowning, she retraced her steps to the staircase and hurried downstairs to the small dining room where the family ate breakfast. Maybe she'd find her father there.

The second she opened the doors, she received a shock. Her sister stood at the antique huntboard pouring herself a cup of coffee.

"Dea! What a surprise! It's good to see you!" She looked beautiful as usual in a stunning blue dress and high heels. Alessandra rushed over to hug her. "Where's Papà?"

"In the office."

"I didn't know you were coming home." She reached for a glass of juice and a roll.

"Neither did I until I got a phone call from him last night."

"You did?" That was news to Alessandra. He must have called her on his way to Metaponto.

Dea's eyes darted to her without warmth. "He told me Rinieri Montanari had come to the castle to do business with him and wanted to know if I had been dating him. He seemed concerned enough that I decided to make a quick trip home to talk to him about it."

"He's always trying to protect us, you know that."

They both sat down at the banquet-size table.

"What I'm curious about is how *you* know Rinieri Montanari." The tone of her sister's point-blank question had an edge. There had to be another reason her sister had made a sudden flight home. Alessandra didn't begin to understand what was going on.

"I don't! Didn't Papà tell you? Signor Montanari was in the foyer when I came in from my scuba-diving trip yesterday. As I started up the staircase he called out to me. I had no idea who he was. He thought I was you."

"Did he say anything else?"

"Only that he acted surprised you were here at the castle and commented that you'd cut your hair since he'd been with you on the yacht. He said you'd told him you had another show to do in Rome. I took it that's why he seemed shocked to find you here. I told him I wasn't you, then I went up the staircase. That's it."

Dea sipped her coffee slowly. "So he mentioned the yacht."

"Yes."

She could hear her sister's mind working. "Is that *all* he told you?"

Dea sounded so worried, Alessandra was perplexed. "I swear it."

Her sister's mouth tightened.

"Have you worked this out with Papà?"

She put down her empty cup. "Not yet, but I will when we fly back to Metaponto in a few minutes."

"But you just got here last night!"

"I have to return to Rome for another show. As soon as Papà finishes up business with Signor Montanari, he's flying me to the airport." She checked her watch. "They've been together for the last half hour."

With nothing more forthcoming, Alessandra knew she'd been dismissed and rose to her feet, feeling chilled. "Then I'll say goodbye to you now." She leaned over to kiss her cheek.

Until Alessandra could talk to her father alone, she would have to wait to know what had gone on. Dea was going back to Rome without clarifying anything about her relationship with Rinieri Montanari. In fact she hadn't been this cold to Alessandra in a long time.

She left the dining room without saying anything and rushed down the hallway to the library, where she could get to work.

When her phone rang two hours later, she saw that it was her father and clicked on. "Papà? Where are you?"

"At the airport in Metaponto, waiting for your mother. She's flying in from Taranto."

Thank goodness. Alessandra needed to talk to her. "Has Dea gone back to Rome?"

"After our talk this morning I put her on the plane."

"You sound more calmed down. Is everything okay?"

"There was a misunderstanding that was all my fault, but I've spoken with Signor Montanari and it's been cleared up."

Except that Alessandra still knew next to nothing. She gripped her phone tighter. "I'm relieved for that. How did Dea seem? She was chilly with me."

"That's because I upset her. After I apologized for minding her business, I explained it was my way of being protective to prevent her from being hurt in case Signor Montanari wasn't being sincere. You did absolutely nothing wrong, so don't worry about it. Now the main reason for my call. Do you have plans for the rest of the day?"

"I'm working on my book."

"Would you have time to do me a favor?"

"Of course."

"Signor Montanari is going to be our guest for the next few days."

What? Alessandra almost fell out of her chair. The change in his attitude toward the other man was astounding.

"He needs someone knowledgeable to show him around today. Since I don't know how long I'm going to be gone, you're the only one I trust to drive him and answer his questions. Your work with the institute has given you vital insight into the importance of any changes or disturbances to the environment here in the south. Will you do it?"

His compliment warmed her heart, but it was already getting a workout because it meant she would be spending time with a man whose name was renowned throughout Italy. Her father had yet to explain what he'd found out about Dea's relationship with Signor Montanari.

"Yes." But Alessandra was so attracted to him, she would have to be careful it didn't show. No way would she give her sister a reason to suspect her of coming on to him when she'd met him first.

"Get him back in time, *piccola*. I've asked him to join us for dinner. Liona has put him in the guest apartment on the third floor. He's probably eating lunch right now. Your mother's plane is arriving so I have to get off the phone. *A piu tarde, figlia mia.*"

* * *

Rini had just finished a second cup of coffee when the beautiful woman he'd seen yesterday on the stairs walked in the dining room. He should have realized right away that she wasn't quite as slender as Dea, but he preferred her curves. "Signor Montanari? I'm sorry if I've kept you waiting. I'm Alessandra." She sounded slightly out of breath and looked flushed.

Earlier in the morning, after the count had asked him about his relationship with Dea, he'd left the castle for the airport. Rini thought it odd to be questioned about her, but he let it go.

At that point the count said that while he was gone, his daughter Alessandra would give him a tour of the property. According to him, she understood the impact of drilling on the environment better than anyone else and he would be in the best of hands. If she was an engineer, Rini had yet to find out.

He got up from the table. "We meet again. I've never met identical twins before."

"Dea's the older sister by three minutes."

"Which accounts for the difference," he teased. "I can see that." He smiled and walked toward her. "Call me Rini."

After a slight hesitation she shook the hand he extended. "*Benvenuto a Posso*, Rini. Papà told me you'd be our guest for a few days and asked me to show you around today."

"That's very kind of you, but I don't want to inconvenience you." He couldn't read her thoughts.

"It's all right. Papà said this was important."

She'd dressed in a simple short-sleeved peach top and jeans. Her tanned olive skin indicated she spent a lot of time in the sun. His gaze traveled from her cognac-brown eyes to her neck-length slightly tousled brown hair rippled through with golden highlights.

As she pulled her hand away, he noticed she didn't wear nail polish. The reason she looked so natural was her lack of makeup. Except that she did wear lipstick, a coral color that blended with the golden tone of her skin and drew his attention to her voluptuous mouth.

He remembered Dea's mouth being sculpted the same way before she'd kissed him. How remarkable that identical twins could look so much alike, yet on closer inspection were so different.

"Your father said you're the one who knows everything."

"Oh, dear. I hope he really didn't say it like that."

Rini got the idea he'd embarrassed her. "He meant it as a compliment."

"I'm his daughter so he has to say it," she commented in a self-deprecating manner. "If you're ready, we can go now."

"Please lead the way."

He followed her ultrafeminine figure out of the castle to a Land Rover parked near the main doors. Rini had done his homework. Her island home was renowned as an Italian treasure. What a coincidence the castle was home to both women!

Before Rini could credit it, she climbed in the driver's seat. "You'll need to move the seat back all the way to accommodate your legs," she said after he opened the passenger door.

One corner of his mouth lifted as he did her bidding and climbed in. They attached their seat belts and she took off across the causeway to the mainland. She drove with expertise, as if she could do it blindfolded. After leaving the small town of Metaponto, they headed for verdant hills that were covered in ancient olive groves.

"My father explained why you're here. Now that we're on Caracciolo property, tell me why the CEO of Montanari Engineering wants to lease this particular piece of property in order to drill. A lease means taking on a lot of controls." She didn't mince words and was all business.

"Your land may not be for sale, but a lease means compromise that benefits both parties and could be lucrative." Rini looked out over the mountainous, sparsely populated province of Basilicata. "Hidden in the arch of Italy's agricultural boot is the home to Europe's biggest on-shore oil field."

"That's what I've heard."

"Italy produces one hundred and twelve thousand barrels a day, one tenth the North Sea's level. My goal is to double Italian oil production within the next five years. If not on your land, then I'll find others because as you know, the south is underdeveloped."

"Your goals are very ambitious."

"Agreed, but the potential of this particular untapped oil field is huge. We're hoping to drill for the billion-plus barrels of crude oil that lie beneath it. Your father and I are hammering out ideas to preserve the existing environment while drilling for oil to boost the suffering Italian economy."

"You sound like a politician."

"Everyone should be concerned over our country's unemployment problems. I'm particularly anxious for us to bring down the country's twelve-percent jobless rate through new employment. The goal will be to obtain oil, yet maintain sustainable development of agriculture that will offer real career paths for the future."

"I have to admit you make a good case." She kept driving to the top of a ridge that overlooked the huge valley. Onorato Caracciolo was a clever man to send Rini out with his daughter first. Rini had a hunch it would be a smart idea to win her over to his idea since her father appeared to place great trust in her knowledge and intelligence. But after the misunderstanding involving his other daughter, he needed to walk carefully.

"If you wouldn't mind stopping, I'd like to get out and look around."

She pulled off the road and turned off the engine. While he walked a ways, she climbed down and rested one curving hip against the front fender to wait for him. When he returned she said, "I know you see oil beneath the property. But what I see is a fertile field that has been here for centuries. Your plan would create giant, unsightly scabs."

His eyes narrowed on the features of her beautiful oval bone structure. "If you're imagining dozens of derricks, you'd be wrong. My gut instinct is to build several right here in the shadow of the mountain out of sight. The existing road to the south travels straight to the sea, where the oil would be transported to tankers. One would barely be aware of the activity."

"And if you find it, does that mean more derricks?"

"We'll make that decision later."

Her softly rounded chin lifted. "What if you don't discover any?"

"Preliminary reports from this part of Italy indicate vast reserves. We'll find it, but we'll proceed slowly with your father having the final say in how long we are allowed to drill. Let me ask you a question."

"Go ahead."

"If I were to appeal to Queen Joanna herself and explain the benefits, what do you propose she would say? Forget how long ago she ruled. Your father tells me you're a historian writing a biography on her. Your research means you know her better than any other living person today. Was she a risk taker?"

He could hear her mind working.

"She backed Antipope Clement VII against the unpopular Urban VI. For that she was given this papally owned land eventually bequeathed to our family. So yes, I'd say she was a risk taker."

Rini's lips twitched—he was fascinated by the knowledge inside her brain. "You think she would have granted me an audience?"

She stared at him. "I have no idea."

"Humor me and put yourself in Joanna's place."

A smile broke the corners of her mouth he found more and more enticing. "It was a man's world. I wouldn't have trusted any of them. You, particularly, wouldn't have been given a second audience."

"Why single me out?"

"Because you're handsome as the devil, increasing the odds of Joanna being tricked. Give me a little more time to think about your ideas that have persuaded my father to give you a hearing."

"You mean you're not tossing me out on my ear just yet?"

She opened the driver's door. "Of course not. That's for Papà to do." On that note she climbed in and started the engine.

He went around to the other side, glad to hear she wasn't shutting him down yet. "In that case, let's take the road that leads to the sea. En route you can tell me more about the subject of your future best seller."

"I'd rather you gave me more reasons why you think this project of yours outweighs the many negatives. My father will want a report to run by my mother and her sister, Fulvia. The property comes through my father's line, but he always leans heavily on the opinions of his wife and sister-in-law."

"Who makes the ultimate decisions?"

"When it comes to business, the three of them go back and forth until there's a consensus."

"He's a man surrounded by women."

She smiled. "As my Aunt Fulvia says, behind every successful man *is* a more successful woman."

Food for thought. "Do your parents love each other?"

"Very much."

"That's nice. Before my mother died, my parents had the same kind of relationship."

"I'm sorry for your loss. It sounds like you've been lucky to have great parents too," she murmured on a sincere note as they started down into the valley. "What does *your* father think of this latest idea of yours?"

"Though he and I are always in consultation over business, this is one time when he doesn't know where I am, or why." He angled his head toward her lovely profile. "I've taken this time to do reconnaissance work on my own. I told no one where I was going, not even my best friend. That's why I was so surprised when I thought you were Dea. I couldn't figure out how you could have known my destination."

She darted him a questioning glance. "So it really was pure coincidence that you had business with our father?"

"I was introduced to her as Dea Loti. But the misunderstanding has been cleared up. The simple fact is, I thought you were she. But I shouldn't have called out to you before I'd met with your father for an explanation, then none of this would have happened. To be honest, I wasn't ready for you to disappear on me the way you did."

Her pulse sped up. *Did he just say what she thought he said?*

"I was a mess and hoped no one would see me sneak in the castle."

"Not from where I was standing."

She swallowed hard and appeared to grip the wheel tighter. "When Dea and I were younger, we got taken for each other a lot. Not so much now that she's become a top fashion model. She's the true beauty. I've always believed I looked different even though we're identical. But I'm aware other people can't always tell the difference. Under the circumstances I understand why my shorter hair gave you a shock."

Not just her hair. As he was coming to learn, many things about her were different from her sister and other women. She was so genuine and charming, it knocked him sideways. "Your hair is attractive and suits you."

"Thank you."

"I can see why your father wants to protect you." Rini decided not to argue the point further when her physical beauty was self-evident. But Alessandra Caracciolo had been born a twin and he'd heard it could be a blessing and a curse, so he left it alone.

They'd reached a crossroads that would take them back to Metaponto and the causeway, but Rini wasn't ready to go home yet. To his surprise he found he wanted to get to know her better. *Much better.* Besides her intelligence, she spoke her mind and was like a breath of fresh air. "Do you have time to drive us along the coast? I want to inspect the shipping access."

"We could do that, but if you want to get a real feel, you should view everything by boat."

That idea sounded much better. "When we reach Metaponto, let's find a marina where I can charter one for tomorrow."

"You don't need to do that. I'm sure my father will want to take you out on our cruiser so you can talk business."

"Then let me buy you dinner in town in order to repay you for driving me around today."

"Thank you, but that's not necessary. My parents are expecting you to eat with them and I have plans after we get back."

He had no right to be disappointed that she'd

just turned him down. She was probably involved in a relationship right now. Why not? She was a stunning woman. He imagined that men flocked to her.

After having shown him around the property for her father, she'd done her duty and had other things to do. Though it was none of his business, for some odd reason the possibility of her being interested in another man didn't sit well with him.

Wednesday morning Alessandra was just getting out of the shower when her phone rang. She reached for her cell and checked the caller ID. "Mamma?"

"*Buongiorno*, darling."

"I'm so glad you're back home. How's Zia Fulvia?"

"I thought she was better. That's why I came home yesterday. But after your father and I finished having dinner with Signor Montanari last evening, we got a call from her. She's having a bad reaction to her new pain medication and it has frightened her. I told her we'd fly to see her this morning. Your father and I are on our way to the airport and will stay with her for another night to watch over her."

"I can't believe you've already gone," Alessandra said in surprise. "I haven't even seen you yet." She needed to talk to her.

"I know. Where did you disappear to last evening? I expected you to join us for dinner."

"I'm behind on my book. After I brought Signor Montanari back to the castle, I went straight to the library to work."

Before Signor Montanari's explanation about Dea, Alessandra had tried hard to hide her attraction to him. But once she knew he and her sister were not involved and never had been, the news had thrilled her so much, she might have given herself away if she'd gone to dinner with him.

"I'm sorry we missed you, darling. I want to hear all about your scuba-diving trip, but it will have to wait another day." Alessandra had already forgotten about that. "Your aunt is really distressed."

"The poor thing. Give her my love and tell her I'll visit her soon."

"She'll love that. By the way, your father wants to know if you would be willing to show Signor Montanari around again? Today he wants to explore the coast by boat. Would you take him out on the cruiser?"

She sucked in her breath. "First let me ask you a question, Mom. What do you think about his idea to lease the property for drilling?"

"To be honest, I don't like the idea at all."

"I didn't think so."

"It seems a travesty to change anything about the land or what lies beneath it. Your father knows how I feel. Though your father believes Signor Montanari's ideas have merit, I'm not persuaded. There's a great deal to discuss before anything is decided."

"It sounds like Papà doesn't feel as strongly as you."

"Let's put it this way. He likes Signor Montanari's vision and is willing to hear more. What's your opinion?"

"He talked a lot about bolstering the economy by providing more jobs. My suspicion is that he's hoping to run for a high-level government position and this could be the feather in his cap."

"He's a brilliant man. That's what brilliant men do." *But not with Caracciolo land.* That's what her mother was really saying. The time Alessandra had spent with him yesterday had persuaded her he was worth listening to, but these were early days. "Alessandra? What's wrong? You don't sound yourself."

"I just wish I hadn't brought Dea into the conversation when I was talking with Papà. He ended up phoning her."

"Your father told me what happened. But when he learned that Signor Montanari had been a guest of Leonides Rossano on his yacht the other night and happened to get introduced to Dea, your father realized he'd made something out of nothing and overreacted. It certainly didn't have anything to do with you."

"But I didn't know the truth until Signor Montanari told me as much while I was driving him around."

"I'm sorry. It's understandable you thought he and your sister were involved."

"I didn't know. When I saw Dea at breakfast yesterday, she didn't explain anything."

"Well he made it clear to your father that meeting Dea was like ships passing in the night."

"But maybe Dea had hopes it could be more." Already Alessandra knew a man like Rinieri Montanari only came along once in a lifetime. She and Dea weren't twins for nothing.

"Why do you say that?"

"If their chance meeting had been so insignificant, how come she flew home last night?"

"Because your father was worried."

"He was," she conceded. "But she didn't even come in my room to talk to me."

"Alessandra—during dinner I got the impression that the CEO of Montanari Engineering is a force to contend with. If he'd been interested in your sister, he would have made future plans to let her know how he felt."

"You're right, but what if she finds out I'm showing him around?"

"What if she does?" After a silence, she asked, "You're attracted to him, aren't you? Otherwise you wouldn't think twice about this. There's nothing wrong with that! I'll admit my heart skipped several beats when I met him at dinner last night."

Her mother's instincts were never wrong.

"He said he truly enjoyed being shown around by you. I could tell he meant it. Don't blow up a simple misunderstanding your father has apologized for into something major."

"You're right. I'm being foolish."

"You are. Go ahead and show Signor Montanari around until we get back from Taranto. I'll call you tonight."

"Okay. Love you. Give Zia Fulvia a hug from me."

Alessandra hung up, realizing she was transparent to her mother, who understood the situation completely. She felt better after their talk. The longing to be with Signor Montanari again was all she could think about.

She pulled on a pair of pleated khaki pants and a blouse with a small tan-on-white geometric print. Once dressed, she went downstairs to the kitchen for coffee and a roll. The cook made her some eggs. While she ate, Liona poked her head in the door. "Alessandra? Did you see Alfredo when you came down the stairs?"

"No."

"He ate his food, but now I can't find him. He usually stays on the main floor while I'm working around. Maybe he's gone off sick somewhere."

"I'll look for him." She ate a last bite, thanked

the cook, then began a search, wondering if Signor Montanari was around. "Alfredo—" She called his name several times. When she reached the front foyer, she worried that he'd slipped past some visitor at the entrance.

She opened the door and almost ran into the gorgeous man who'd haunted her dreams. He was just coming in. The sight of him made her heart leap. He held the big marmalade cat in his arms.

"*Buongiorno*, Alessandra," he said with a white smile. "I've been waiting for a limo and found him lying outside the door wanting to get back in."

"Liona will be so relieved. Here. I'll carry him to the kitchen."

"I'll be happy to do it."

"I don't mind."

She could tell he didn't want to give up the cat, who seemed perfectly happy to be held by him. It surprised her because Alfredo didn't like many people. "Then follow me." She opened the door and showed him the way.

Liona was thrilled to see them walk in the kitchen. The housekeeper reached for her cat.

"He found Alfredo outside the castle," Alessandra explained.

"The poor thing is getting confused. I'll take him back to my apartment. *Grazie, signor.*"

"*Prego, signora.*"

Alessandra trailed him out of the kitchen. "That was very nice of you. Her cat is getting old." She followed him to the entrance, but there was no sign of a limo yet, only three tour buses bringing tourists to tour the part of the castle open to the public. "I hope the driver didn't already come and leave."

"I'll call to find out." He reached in his jeans pocket. Her eyes traveled over his rock-hard body. His blue crewneck shirt had the kind of short sleeves that only looked good on a man with a well-defined physique. In a minute he clicked off. "It'll be a while due to an accident near the causeway."

"What were your plans?"

His veiled gaze slid to hers. "To charter a boat."

"There's no need to do that," she said on impulse. "Since my father isn't here to take you, he suggested I drive you where you want to go in our cruiser."

"But that means interrupting your work."

"It's all right. As Papà reminded me, you're a busy man. Since you're here, you need to make the most of the time. I'll do my own work later." The talk with Alessandra's mother had taken away the guilt she'd been harboring over Dea. There was nothing she wanted more than to spend more time with him.

"Then I'll call off the limo."

"While you do that, I have to run in and get a few things. I'll meet you at the Land Rover in five minutes."

Alessandra hurried inside and up the staircase to her room. Her heart raced abnormally hard to think they were going out on the boat together. She filled her duffel bag with some necessary items, then rushed back down to the kitchen and stashed water and snacks in the top of it. She never knew how long she'd be gone, so she never left without being prepared.

When she walked out to the car beneath a semicloudy sky, she found him waiting for her with his own backpack. It had been years since she'd felt this alive around a man. This time when she unlocked the door with the remote, he opened her door and relieved her of her duffel bag so she could get in. He walked on around and put their things in the back before climbing inside.

"Our cruiser is docked on the other side of the island." She started the engine and drove them the short distance.

"It's right in your backyard!"

She smiled. "I know. Can you believe how convenient?"

Once she'd pulled up to the pier, they both got out. He obviously knew his way around a boat. After depositing their bags, he undid the ropes while she got on board and found them both life preservers. She put hers on first.

"Who's the scuba enthusiast?"

"You're looking at her."

His piercing dark brown eyes scrutinized her. "How long have you been a diver?"

"Since I was nineteen. Have you ever done it?"

"I learned at fourteen. It's probably my favorite activity."

His admission excited her no end. To scuba dive with him would be like a dream come true. "Mine, too," she admitted. "Excuse me for a minute."

She disappeared below and pulled out a special oceanography chart of the area for him to look at. When she came up on deck she discovered he'd climbed on board and had put on his preserver. "Here." She put the rolled-up chart on the banquette next to him. "You can look at this as we proceed." Alessandra started the engine at a wakeless speed and drove them toward open water.

"This cruiser is state of the art."

She nodded. "A huge change from our old boat I took everywhere until my father bought this for me so I could go on longer trips."

"For pleasure?"

"It's always a pleasure, but I'm part of a team working for the Institute of Archaeological and Monumental Heritage."

Her response seemed to surprise him. "Where did you go to college?"

"I received my master's degree from the University of Catania. Our job is to identify and retrieve buried structures of archaeological interest."

"Living on an archaeological wonder, you come by your interest naturally."

She nodded. "My area of academics is to study the advanced techniques for nondestructive testing and remote sensing. Hopefully our work will expand our knowledge and help restore the historical buildings above and below the water in this area of Italy."

He sat on the banquette across from her with his hands clasped between his knees. She felt his eyes probing her with new interest. "It's no wonder your father told me I would be in good hands with you. You're an archaeologist. I thought maybe you were an engineer.

"Your father knew that you're exactly the person I need to consult while I'm here. Like you, I'm anxious to identify where the drilling will cause the least amount of destruction to the environment, both on land and water."

"Tell you what. After I give you a tour of the coastline, we'll go to my office at the castle. Since you're an engineer, you can watch a series of videos we've produced that will open your eyes to the many roadblocks you'll have to consider in order to drill and transport oil."

"I'm indebted to you, Alessandra."

"You have no idea what kinds of snags you're up against, so don't get too excited, *signore*."

"Call me Rini," he urged for a second time in his deep male voice that affected her insides. "I like snags. They make life exciting."

Though she agreed with him, she needed to be careful not to let this man get under her skin. Alessandra had a hunch he wasn't just talking about the search for oil. He had a way of infiltrating her defenses no matter where she turned. She had a feeling that if she got involved with him, he had the power to hurt her in ways that she would never get over.

"Why don't you consult the map I brought up? It will explain a lot as we go."

As they cruised along the coast, she glimpsed a half smile that broke the corner of his compelling mouth before he did her bidding and unraveled it for his perusal. He was such a breathtaking man, she could hardly concentrate.

It was hard to believe he wanted to be with her and not Dea. For some reason Rini Montanari hadn't been interested in her sister. She couldn't comprehend it.

Probably Dea hadn't been able to comprehend it, either. But Alessandra didn't know what went on in her sister's mind and would be a fool to make any more assumptions about anything.

Just be excited that he wants to be with you, Alessandra.

CHAPTER THREE

BY FIVE IN the afternoon Rini had seen as much as he needed for a preliminary assessment. Alessandra had been a fountain of knowledge. Depending on Onorato's willingness to continue their talks, he wanted to bring out a team from the Naples office to begin an in-depth exploration.

But at this point business wasn't on his mind. During their outing he'd grown hungry. She'd brought along water and snacks, but he wanted a big dinner and intended to surprise her by taking her out for a meal. He'd seen a helipad at the side of the castle and went below deck to call for a helicopter.

With her expertise she guided the boat to the pier and shut off the engine. He discarded the life preserver and jumped to the dock to tie the ropes. In a moment the rotors of the helicopter sounded overhead.

Alessandra looked up. "I guess my parents are back. That's a surprise. Mother told me they could be gone for several days." She removed her preserver.

"I think that's *my* helicopter."

She blinked. "You sent for yours?" Did he see disappointment in her eyes?

"I chartered one to take us to dinner. Last night you turned me down. Tonight I decided not to take any chances on another rejection."

Her eyes slid away from his. "Where are we going?"

Good. She'd decided not to fight him. "That's my surprise. Bring what you need and leave the rest in the boat. We'll retrieve everything later."

"You don't want to change clothes?"

"There's no need."

She nodded. "I'll only be a moment." Before

long she came back up on deck having applied a fresh coat of lipstick.

Avoiding his help, she climbed out of the boat and they made their way to the helicopter in the distance. But she couldn't refuse him when he opened the door to assist her into the back. Their arms brushed and he inhaled her light, flowery fragrance, which made him more aware of her.

Within seconds they lifted off and the pilot flew them due east. For the next little while her gaze fastened on the landscape below. When they started their descent to the city of a hundred thousand, she darted Rini an excited glance. "I love Lecce! It's a masterpiece of baroque architecture."

"I haven't been here in several years, but I remember a restaurant near the cathedral and hope it's still as good."

He'd arranged for a limo to drive them into the city nicknamed the Florence of the South. They got out and started walking along the narrow, shop-lined streets to the square for their dinner.

Lots of tourists, plus music from the many eating places, put him in a holiday spirit, something he hadn't felt in years. Alessandra stopped in front of every shop and boutique, all of which were made from the soft local limestone. The facades were a mass of cherubs. She delighted in their faces as well as the displays. He hadn't felt this carefree in years.

"Oh, Rini. Look at that precious cat! It reminds me of Alfredo." They'd stopped in front of a souvenir shop selling the famous *Cartapesta* items of saints and animals made out of papier-mâché and painted.

"I think you're right. Let's buy it for your housekeeper." Without waiting for a response, he lifted the three-inch orange crouching cat from the shelf and walked inside to pay for it. The clerk put it in a sack. When he exited the shop, Alessandra stared up at him.

"She'll be thrilled."

He handed her the gift. "Will you keep it until we get back to the castle?"

"That was very kind of you," she said in a quiet voice. After sliding it in her purse, they walked out to the square.

"If my memory serves me correctly, our restaurant is on the right, halfway down the colonnade. We'll eat what they bring us. There's no menu." After the call to arrange for the helicopter, he made a reservation at the famous restaurant. When they reached it, the maître d' showed them inside to a table that looked out on the square.

Mugs of *caffé in ghiaccio con latte di mandorla* arrived. She smiled between sips. "I'm already addicted to that wonderful almond flavor."

"Agreed. How about the antipasto?"

She experimented. "These are fabulous. I could make a whole meal on the salmon-and-oyster bruschetta alone."

"I like the little tortillas with olives."

"There's nothing not to like, Rini." Soon they were served angel-hair pasta with sardines. If that wasn't enough, they were brought mouth-watering apple crostinos for dessert.

"I'm so full, I don't think I can move. Thank you for bringing us here. I haven't had a meal like this in years."

He loved it that she enjoyed her food. "It's the least I can do after everything you've done for me. I'm in awe of your knowledge. Not only that, you're a master sea woman." He put some bills on the table, then got up and escorted her out of the restaurant. Night had fallen, adding to the beauty of the square.

"A *sea woman*? Sounds like a new species." Her soft laughter charmed him.

"Until your father gets back, I'm hoping to spend a few more days on the water with you. It's true I'm here on business, but I've decided to take a few days to mix pleasure with it."

He led them through a street to find a taxi so they could head back to the helipad at the airport. Once on board they took off, then he turned to her. "Your scuba equipment has been calling to me. How about we pick up some gear for me tomorrow and you take us where you go diving. I'll charter us a boat."

"That would be ridiculous when we can use my boat."

"I wouldn't want you to think I'm taking advantage of you."

"Can we just not worry about that?"

"That's fine with me. What I'd like to do is camp out. I'll be your buddy. Could I tear you away from your work that long, or would it be asking too much?"

After they reached the island and got in the car, she eyed him speculatively. "After the exquisite meal, it pains me to have to turn you down. I'm afraid I'm behind on my project, but you're welcome to take the cruiser and go exploring on your own."

He didn't believe her excuse. She could be warm and engaging, but if he got too close, she'd retreat. After finally meeting a woman who thrilled him in so many ways, he couldn't take the disappointment that she put other plans first. It was driving him crazy.

"If you don't go with me, I won't have a buddy. You're so smart and know so much, a trip without you wouldn't be fun. What if we go out early after your work is over for the day? Say two o'clock?"

"I'm not sure I can be finished by then." She got out of the car and started walking to the entrance in an attempt to elude him.

He caught up to her. "Then we'll play it by ear."

"You never give up, do you?" But she said it with a smile. "All right."

Those two little words gave him hope, but the minute they went inside the castle, Liona and her cat were there to greet them. "You have a visitor, Alessandra. He insisted on waiting for you. I've put him in the small salon."

Him? Maybe Rini had been right and she was seeing someone.

"Thank you, Liona." She pulled the sack out of her purse. "This is for you. Signor Montanari bought it for you."

The older woman smiled. *"Veramente?"* She opened the sack and pulled out the cat. "This looks like *you*, Alfredo. You must have bought this in Lecce!"

Rini nodded. "It caught our eye."

"Mille grazie, signor. Come on, Alfredo. Let's look at this treasure together." She put the cat in her arms. *"Buona notte,"* she called over her shoulder.

Alessandra's eyes darted to him. "You've made her night."

He cocked his head. "But it appears yours isn't over yet, so I'll leave you to your guest and see you tomorrow. *Dormi bene.*"

After wishing her good-night he headed for the stairs, which he took two at a time to his room on the third floor. Full of adrenaline because she'd finally agreed to be with him to-morrow, he pulled out his phone and returned Guido's call. Though it was late, his friend would probably still be awake. On the third ring he answered.

"Rini? I'd given up and was headed for bed."

"Sorry. I just got back to my room."

"Where are you?"

"In a castle on the island of Posso."

Guido chuckled. "Sure you are. So what's happening? Are we still on for Saturday?"

"I'm not sure."

"Don't tell me it's work again."

"Not this time."

"That sounds serious."

"I am. Have you got a minute?"

"Since when do you have to ask me a question like that? Go ahead. I'm all ears."

For the next little while he unloaded on his friend, leaving nothing out. When he'd finished, Guido whistled in response.

"In my gut I know Alessandra likes me, but

she's keeping me at a distance. I asked her to go scuba diving tomorrow and she finally gave in, but she's not easy to understand. She doesn't wear a ring, but tonight a man was waiting for her when we got back from dinner."

"Then the first thing you need to find out is if she's committed."

Rini's brows furrowed. "I don't think she is. The housekeeper referred to the man as a visitor."

"All's fair then. Are you thinking she's being hesitant because you met her sister first? You know, that kind of unwritten law thing."

"Maybe."

"The only way to find out is go after her and learn the truth for yourself."

"I'll do it. Thanks for the advice."

After a long silence, his friend said, "I've been wondering when this day would come."

Guido wasn't the only one...

"I'll call you later in the week to make final plans for Saturday. Ciao."

He rang off, but he was feeling restless and decided to go for a walk before trying to get some sleep.

Alessandra waited outside the castle entrance while Bruno drove to the dock to get his scuba gear. When he came back, she approached the driver's side of his van. "Did you find everything?"

He nodded. "I'm sorry to have bothered you so late. I have to leave on the diving trip for the institute in the morning. I wish you'd join us. We'll be out there for another three days at least."

"What spot this time?"

"The same one. We haven't begun to explore that area thoroughly."

"I agree."

"Will you come? I know you're busy on your book, but we need your expertise." His gray eyes urged her to say yes. "I'd rather buddy with you than anyone else."

I know. But she didn't feel the same. "Bruno? Please don't take this wrong, but I want to keep our friendship on a professional basis and won't be buddying with you again."

He looked surprised. "Does this mean there's someone else?"

Exasperated, she said, "It means I'd prefer to keep my work separate from my personal life. I hope you understand."

Tight-lipped, he accelerated faster than necessary and took off.

"Someone didn't seem very happy," a deep male voice said behind her.

She whirled around in shock. "Rini, I—I thought you'd gone to bed."

"It's a beautiful night. I was afraid I wouldn't be able to sleep, so I decided to go for a walk around the castle. Did the fact that my kidnapping you to Lecce upset certain plans you had with your visitor?"

"If I'd had plans, I wouldn't have gone with you. That man was Dr. Tozzi from the archaeological institute. He came to get his scuba gear out of the cruiser. Tomorrow he's going on another exploratory dive with the others for a few days."

"You two dive together a lot?"

"There's a whole group of us. Last week we went out on our boats from Metaponto. He happened to be my buddy that trip, so that's why his scuba gear ended up in the cruiser. Tonight I told him he'd have to find another buddy because I would like our relationship to stay completely professional. "

"He doesn't have his own boat?"

"Yes, but he forgot to transfer his equipment after we'd finished. The institute has a state-of-the-art oceanography boat, but he won't bring it out until we've made a positive find."

"I see. Are you supposed to go out with them again?"

"Yes, but I have to divide up my time."

His dark brows lifted. "You're a very important person, besieged on every side, so I have an idea for tomorrow. While you work on your book for part of the day, I'll run in to Metaponto to get me some gear. Then we'll join your group. En route you and I can talk over your father's business. That way you can please everyone, including me. What do you say?"

She let out a sigh. Already he was reducing her to mush. "I'll get up early and work until lunch, then we'll leave for Metaponto. The dive shop will have the gear you need. From there we can head for the dive site and meet up with the others."

"I'd like to stay out overnight and camp."

"I would, too. It's one of my favorite things to do."

"Good." His eyes blazed. "I shall look forward to it. I'll see you at lunch."

He took off for another run around the tiny island without giving her a chance to say anything else. Alessandra hurried inside the castle, secretly excited to go diving with him. Thoughts of buddying with him left her breathless. The idea that they would protect each other was so appealing she couldn't wait.

At six the next morning she showered and dressed quickly before heading to the library to work on her book. While she was knee-deep in research, Liona entered the library.

"Alessandra? Signor Montanari is eating his lunch in the dining room."

Her head lifted. "It's that time already?"

"*Si.* One o'clock."

"I can't believe I lost track of time. Tell him I'll be right there."

She raced out of the room and up the stairs to freshen up, then hurried back down with her packed duffel bag. When she entered the dining room he stood up to greet her. The man looked amazing in white cargo pants and a dark brown crewneck shirt.

"Sorry I'm late."

His dark eyes traveled up her jean-clad legs to her white pullover, then found her gaze. "We're in no hurry. Sit down and eat lunch."

"I'd rather not take the time now. While you rent scuba gear, I'll grab us some food and drinks at the nearby deli to hold us over until tomorrow."

"With the announcement of an overnight on the water, you've made my day, *signorina.*"

Everything he said and did made her pulse race. Her feelings for him were spilling all over the place. She didn't know how to stop them. *She didn't want to stop them.*

He followed her out of the room with his backpack and they left for Metaponto in the cruiser. At the dive shop they loaded up with extra tanks. Once they'd bought drinks and groceries, they gassed up the cruiser and headed west. She handed him the special ocean chart he'd looked at before.

"We'll be diving at the midway point between Metaponto and Crotone. Some of the finds date back to the Magna Graecia. We're looking for some columns from the sixth century before Christ reputed to be there.

"If we're really lucky, we'll see the remnants of a temple dedicated to the goddess Hera. This area of the Ionian is a treasure trove, but as you realize, all the artifacts are buried, making them almost impossible to discover."

Rini looked up from the chart to flash her an intriguing smile. "It's the *almost* impossible that fires your blood, *non è vero?*"

She nodded. But artifacts weren't the only thing that fired her blood. The flesh-and-blood male who was a living Adonis had made her come alive without even trying. She'd taken one look at him that first evening in the castle foyer and had fallen so hard, she feared she would never recover.

It was too late to wish he'd gone back to Naples. Already she hated the idea that he would have to leave at all. Her thoughts were crazy. This was the renowned Rinieri Montanari she was talking about, not just any man.

Alessandra imagined that every woman who met him couldn't get enough. Even her mother had been bowled over by him. But the fact that he was still a bachelor meant there was a big reason he didn't have a wife.

Maybe he'd lost a great love and could never bring himself to marry. Or he enjoyed women, but couldn't commit to one for fear of feeling trapped. So no matter how attentive he was being right now, Alessandra would be a fool to think *she* would be the one woman in Italy who could do what no other female had done and win his love.

She glanced at him. "How long has it been since you went diving?"

Rini folded up the chart. "A year, but don't worry. You can count on me." Deep down she knew she could trust him. He engendered a confidence she'd never felt around other men. It didn't bother her that he'd just said he wasn't concerned about the time that had passed since his last dive.

"How have you stayed away from it so long?"

"Too much work."

"But there are lots of marvelous diving sites in the Naples area. Surely you could have taken some time off."

"True, but even though the office is there, I don't live in Naples and am always anxious to fly home at the end of the day."

That was a surprise. "Where is home?"

"Positano."

"Oh—such a glorious spot with fabulous diving opportunities."

"My friends and siblings did it with me for several years, but for most of the last year my sister Valentina lived with me while she was expecting her baby. That meant no diving for her. As I told you earlier, we'd just lost our mother in a car accident. I divided my time between visiting my father at our family home in Naples and staying around the villa for my sister in order to keep her company."

Alessandra hadn't realized he'd carried such a load. She was touched by the way he cared for his family. "Did she have her baby?"

"*Si.* My nephew, Vito, is thriving. The man Valentina married has adopted him. They live in Ravello with his son, Ric. Both babies were born the same day at the same hospital."

"You're kidding—"

"What's really amazing was that the babies got switched. Valentina brought the wrong baby home while the man she married took home Valentina's son."

"*What?*" She almost lost control of the wheel. "How awful! Where was the mother?"

"They were divorced. At birth she gave up her mother's rights to Giovanni. It was a nightmare after the babies were returned to their birth parents. By then Valentina and Giovanni had bonded with the children. At that point they began to see each other so they could be with both babies and they fell in love."

A smile lit up her face. "That's the greatest love story I ever heard. How hard to love the wrong baby, but how sweet they were able to make everything work out. The person I feel sorry for is the mother who gave her child away. I can't comprehend it. I love my mother so much, I don't want to think what it would have been like if she hadn't been there for me. In fact I can't wait until the day comes when I can have my own baby."

He seemed caught up in his own thoughts before he said, "Fortunately she came to her senses and has now worked out visitation so she can help raise her son."

"That's the way it should be!" But Alessandra couldn't help but wonder about the father of his sister's baby. Still, she didn't want to pry.

"I can read your mind, Alessandra. Vito's father was one of Valentina's engineering professors at the University in Naples, but he didn't want marriage or children. My sister suffered terribly, but today she's so happy, you would never know she'd been through so much trauma."

Alessandra could relate to the trauma. Her hands tightened on the controls. She was living proof you could get through a broken heart and survive the emotional pain, but not everyone could end up as happy as his sister.

"So she's an engineer, too."

"Yes. A brilliant one."

"What does her husband do for a living?"

"He's the CEO of the Laurito Corporation."

Alessandra smiled at him. "That's an amazing combination. Your sister was blessed to have a brother like you to watch over her." She was coming to find out Rini was an extraordinary man. He'd even bought that little gift for Liona.

"Our family is close."

Alessandra could say the same where her parents were concerned. Before long she could pick out the red-and-white scuba flags from two boats ahead. "There they are!" The group had already started diving in an area near the coast. "If anything of significance is found, Dr. Tozzi will bring out the institute's boat. Today we're still exploring."

Alessandra brought her boat to a stop and

lowered the anchor. After she raised her flag, she looked back at Rini. He'd already slipped on his wet suit. By the gleam in his eyes she could tell he'd been anticipating this dive.

"I'll be right back." She took her wet suit below to change. Talk about excited. She could hardly keep her fingers from trembling before going back up on deck.

In a moment they'd put on their weight belts and buoyancy-control devices. He reminded her of the film phenomenon James Bond. She finished dressing and put her goggles in place. "We'll be going down eighty feet. Ready?"

"*Si, bellissima.*"

He shouldn't have said that to her. The deep tone of his compliment curled to her insides, disturbing her concentration. She ended up jumping in the water after he did, almost forgetting to keep her goggles and regulator in place.

The air temperature registered eighty degrees, but the water was cooler. Once below the surface she pressed the button to let out some air. The weights carried her down, down. Rini stayed right with her, watching her as their ears adjusted to the pressure. She could tell by the way he moved that he was a pro. It made her feel perfectly safe.

Eight minutes later they reached the sea floor with its clumps of vegetation and only a smattering of tiny fish. He stayed with her as she moved toward the area where she could see the group working. They all waved to her. She motioned for Rini to swim with her beyond the circle and examine a nearby area. The ridge in the distance looked promising, but as she brushed some of the debris away, it turned out to be more debris instead of a column lying on its side.

Rini found some interesting spots and waved her over to him, but every investigation came up short. She got the feeling they were searching in the wrong area. After a half hour he tapped his watch. She'd been about to do the same thing because it was time to go up and it would take a while.

They started the ascent, listening to the rhythm of their breathing through their regulators. She felt like they were the only people alive and loved this dive that had been magical for her. The sheer pleasure of enjoying this experience with him, of depending on him, could never be equaled.

Once they broke the surface, he helped her onto the transom before levering himself on board. Before she could sit down on a banquette, another boat approached them.

"Alessandra—"

"Ciao, Bruno." She waved to him and the three others from the institute who rode with him.

"I was hoping you'd make it. Who's your friend?"

"Bruno Tozzi, meet Signor Montanari." The two men nodded. She refused to tell him anything about Rini. "It's too bad we haven't turned up anything interesting yet."

"We'll have to keep searching tomorrow."

Another of the divers said, "Why don't you join us in Crotone for dinner?"

"Thank you, but I'm afraid we have other plans. We'll do another dive with you in the morning."

"*Bene.*"

In a minute their boat drove off. Alessandra was glad he'd gone and hurried below deck to get out of her wet suit. When she came up on deck a few minutes, she found Rini already changed into his clothes. He'd organized their gear near the back of the boat and had taken down the flag.

His eyes played over her. "It's growing dark. Do you have a place in mind where we can camp?"

"Yes. A small, secluded cove five minutes from here. I'll raise the anchor." She turned on the boat lights and they headed for the coast. Her heart fluttered in her chest when she thought of spending the night out here with him. Because she knew this area so well, they arrived quickly. She cut the engine and the momentum swept them onto the sandy portion of the isolated beach.

Alessandra turned to him. "Do you want to eat on deck, or in the galley?"

"Since the food is already up here, let's stay put, shall we? I'll do the honors and serve you for a change."

"Well, thank you."

In a minute he had everything laid out on the opposite banquette and they could pick what they wanted—fruit, meat pastries, cheese rolls, drinks, chocolate and almonds.

He sat back in the chair opposite her and feasted. "After that dive, this is heaven," he admitted with satisfaction.

"I can tell you're a seasoned diver, Rini. It was a privilege to be with you today."

"Now you know how I feel to have joined you.

I'm excited about tomorrow's dive. Maybe we'll find something, but even if we don't, it doesn't take away from the thrill of being with an expert like you."

His compliments sounded so sincere, she was in danger of believing them. "I loved it."

After a brief silence, he said, "Dr. Tozzi was upset to see you out here with me, so don't deny it."

"I wasn't going to." She reached for some more grapes. "I'm glad you were with me. I've told him I'm not interested in him. Now he's seen it for himself."

Rini's dark brows furrowed. "Is that the reason I was invited along?"

He couldn't really think that, could he? It would mean he felt vulnerable. She couldn't imagine him having a vulnerable bone in his body. She leaned forward. "Of course not!"

He bit into another plum. "Is there an important man in your life?"

Yes. I'm looking at him. "Not in years."

"Why not?"

"I could ask you the same thing," she blurted without thinking. "Why does Rinieri Montanari sail alone?"

"I asked you first," he returned. "A beautiful, fascinating woman like you has to have a history."

Alessandra wasn't used to hearing those adjectives attributed to herself. If he only knew it, she was totally enamored with him. "You don't really want to know."

"I wouldn't have asked otherwise." At this point he'd put the leftover food back in the sacks she would take down to the galley later.

"I fell in love with Francesco at twenty-two. He was a chef from Catania when I was in my last year of undergraduate school. He swore undying love for me and said he'd found his soul mate. I believed him. We talked about getting married.

"One weekend Dea came to visit. I was excited for her to meet him. She stayed in my apartment with me and the three of us spent time together. After she left for Rome, where she was pursuing a modeling career, everything seemed to change. He suddenly told me he had to go on vacation and would call me as soon as he got back. During those two weeks he didn't phone me once.

"I thought I'd lose my mind until I heard from him. I imagined every reason under the sun for his absence except the one he gave me. He didn't have the decency to tell me in person. Instead, he sent me a letter telling me he'd fallen in love with Dea and knew I couldn't forgive him."

Lines darkened Rini's features in the semidarkness.

"At the time it was terrible. Dea didn't come home for two months. When she did, she told me he'd followed her to Rome, but it was over between the two of them almost before it had begun. She thought he was a loser and told me I was better off without him.

"Though inwardly I agreed, my pain had reached its zenith because Dea always had this power to get the boys interested in her. But when it came to Francesco, who I thought was committed to me, something broke inside me. I suffered for a long time. But it happened over six years ago and is buried in the past." She took a drink of water. "Now it's your turn to tell me the secrets of your heart, dark or otherwise."

CHAPTER FOUR

RINI FELT LIKE he'd been stabbed in the chest. Too many emotions rocked him at once. There was someone he needed to talk to before he bared his soul to Alessandra.

"I'm afraid my story would take all night. Let's reserve it for tomorrow evening after another dive. If you don't mind, I'd like to sleep up here tonight."

"Then you'll need the quilt and pillow on the bed in the other cabin in order to be comfortable."

"I'll get them."

"You sound tired after that dive, Rini. I am too, so I'll say good night."

"*Buona notte.*"

He waited an hour before going below to

bring up the bedding. Once he'd made himself comfortable on the banquette at the rear of the cruiser, he pulled out his phone and called his sister. Rini knew it was too late to be phoning, but he had to talk to her.

After four rings he heard her voice. "Rini? What's wrong? Has something happened to Father?"

"No, no."

After a short silence she asked, "Are you ill?" He could hear Giovanni's concerned voice in the background.

"Not physically. But I'm wrestling with a problem that needs your slant. Do you mind?"

"What a question! After all you've done for me, I'd give anything to help you if I can. Tell me what's going on."

He raised up on one elbow. "Let me give you a little background." Without wasting words, he explained his dilemma from beginning to end.

"Ooh" was all she said when he'd finished.

"Forgive me if this touches too close to home,

but you're the one person in the world who would understand her pain after Francesco went after her sister."

"Rini? I got over Matteo's womanizing and it sounds like she has gotten over her pain, too, so forget her past. You only have one problem. Let this woman know how you feel about her and prove to her that your love for her is everlasting. If Mamma were still alive, she would tell you to follow your heart and not let anything get in the way."

He could hear his mother saying those very words. "Alessandra was really hurt."

"So was I. It passes when the right man comes along. Trust me."

He breathed deeply. "You make it sound so simple."

"Nothing worthwhile is simple, Rini. But look what happened when I followed my heart instead of letting go of Ric, the baby I thought was mine..."

"You mean instead of listening to me tell you

not to get involved with Giovanni," he groaned. "I was a fool to interfere."

"Of course you weren't! I know you were only trying to protect me. But it all worked out and I'm now an ecstatic wife and the mother of two angelic boys."

His eyes closed tightly. "But from the start Giovanni wanted you enough to defy convention, too. That's why it worked."

"Rini, tonight you're alone with her on her family's cruiser. Do you seriously think that would have happened if she weren't absolutely crazy about you?"

"Her father asked her to show me around."

"But to dive? Camp out over night? Have faith, dear brother. A little patience wouldn't hurt until she realizes she can trust you with her life."

A lump had lodged in his throat. "*Ti amo*, Valentina."

"*Ti amo. Buona notte.*"

Rini lay back down, thinking about what

she'd said. Even if a miracle happened and her attraction grew into love, she didn't know about his infertility, an insurmountable hurdle in his mind.

The next thing he knew, the sound of gulls brought him fully awake. Clouds blotted out the sun. He sat up to check his watch. Seven thirty. Was Alessandra still asleep? He gathered the bedding and took it below to the other cabin. Her door was still closed.

One thing he could do was fix them his favorite prosciutto ham and eggs to go with their breakfast. As he was putting their plates and mugs on the table, she appeared in the doorway wearing jeans and a T-shirt that molded to her beautiful body.

"You've got color in your cheeks."

"I went for a walk."

He'd had no idea. What a wonderful body-guard he'd made! "If you'd wakened me, I would have gone with you. Sit down and I'll serve you."

"Umm. Everything smells good."

He poured them coffee and sat opposite her. She took a sip. "How did you sleep?"

Rini stared at her through shuttered eyes. "There's nothing better than spending the night under the stars. What about you?"

"It's fabulous out here, but I confess diving makes me tired. I fell asleep once my head touched the pillow."

"That's good. How soon do we need to join the others?"

"They'll be out there by nine o'clock."

He swallowed the last of his eggs. "Just for the fun of it, what would you think if we enlarged the search area by traveling a quarter of a mile farther east from them to dive at the same distance from the coast?" He wasn't ready to share her with the others yet. "I consulted the chart. The depth of the sea floor isn't quite as great there. Maybe seventy feet. Who knows? We might make a discovery."

Her lips turned up at the corners. "Your mother

must have gone crazy to have a son who went around with such an excited gleam for adventure in his eyes."

Rini liked the idea that she'd noticed. "Is that what I have?"

"Oh, yes. It probably got you into a ton of trouble."

He chuckled. "So what do you say?"

"I like your idea. Later on this afternoon we can join the others for another dive."

"Sounds like a plan." Pleased she was willing to go along with him so they could be alone a little longer, he got to his feet to clean up the kitchen. She cleared the dishes and they made quick work of it. He'd never experienced this kind of togetherness with a woman before. Rini couldn't imagine letting her go.

"Thanks for fixing the delicious breakfast. I'll change into my wet suit and meet you on deck."

He bounded up the stairs to put on his own gear. To spend a whole day with her doing something they both loved couldn't have excited him more.

In fifteen minutes they'd arrived at the spot he'd suggested for a dive. They had the whole sea to themselves for the moment. She lowered the anchor and erected the flag. Together they put on all their equipment. "Ready?" he called to her.

Her brandy eyes clung to his, pulling at his heart strings. "Let's go!"

They jumped in the water. He experienced delight as they sank lower past more tiny fish. Once they reached the bottom, they explored around all the vegetation that grew taller and was more plentiful than at the other spot. He saw traces of some deep-sea-fishing tackle caught by the undergrowth. It was like playing hide-and-seek as they swam here and there like little children let out to play.

His eyes followed her as they moved through a new chute. He was so mesmerized by the fun he was having, he almost ran into her because she'd suddenly stopped. When he looked beyond her, he saw a large roundish shape like a big boulder covered in debris ahead of them.

The hairs lifted on the back of his neck and knew she was feeling the same electricity. Something was here that didn't belong. He swam to one side of it and waited for her to approach the other side. She was the expert.

Her hands began to brush away the layers of silt. He helped her. After five minutes of hard work, they uncovered part of what looked like a sculpted mouth. Alessandra's eyes stared at him with a glow through her goggles. This was a fantastic find and they both knew it.

While he marveled, she tapped her watch. He'd been too engrossed and forgot the time. They needed to go up to the surface now! It was hard to leave after what they'd just discovered, but they would be back later.

Rini knew the rules by heart. Keep his breathing steady as they rose, but it was hard when his adrenaline was gushing. He could only imagine Alessandra's joy. This was her life!

They broke the top of the water and swam toward the boat. Like déjà vu he helped her on board the cruiser, then climbed in himself.

"Oh, Rini," she cried, having removed the belt and breathing apparatus. "We found something that could have belonged to the Temple of Hera. We've got to find Dr. Tozzi and bring the others here!"

Without conscious thought he grasped her upper arms, bringing her close to his body. "Congratulations!"

Her eyes, the color of dark vintage brandy, searched his. "It was your inspiration that brought us here."

For a moment he was caught up in the wonder of her beauty that went soul deep. "I'll never forget the experience of winding through that undersea garden with you."

"Neither will I," she whispered.

He pulled her closer and closed his mouth

close over hers. The unexpectedness of it must have caught her off guard because she began kissing him back with a fervency he could only have dreamed about.

Hungry for her, Rini drove their kiss deeper, marveling over her response to him. Sensation after sensation of desire caused him to kiss her senseless. Only the wake from a passing boat that bounced the cruiser reminded him how far gone he was.

Alessandra seemed to feel it, too. She tore her lips from his and moved out of his arms. "If— if you'll mark this spot on the chart, I'll drive," she stuttered.

He didn't like it that she'd headed for the controls, leaving him bereft. So much for him practicing the patience Valentina had talked about. Rini hadn't been able to keep himself from crushing her in his arms. He'd wanted that divine fusion to go on and on.

While Alessandra raised the anchor and started the engine, he reached in his backpack for a pen. He found the rolled-up chart on the banquette and sat down to fill in the information, but it was difficult. To his surprise the wind had kicked up. He looked overhead and noticed that more clouds had been amassing. Three hours ago it had only been overcast and there hadn't been this breeze.

She drove as fast as the elements would allow. Finally in the distance he saw the flags of the three boats. They drew closer and waved to several groups of divers in two of the boats. Soon Alessandra drew alongside one of them. "How long has Dr. Tozzi been down?"

"He and Gino should be coming up any minute."

"Did you find anything?"

They shook their heads.

"Well, all is not lost. We have some amazing news." She cut the engine and lowered the anchor while they waited in the rocking crafts for the head of the institute to appear. Rini shared a private glance with her. He could feel her eagerness to impart their finding.

Rini watched until he saw two heads pop out of the water. The divers reached their boat and climbed in. The second the good doctor removed his headgear, his gaze shot to Alessandra.

"You missed this morning's dive."

"We did our own dive farther east and raced here to tell you what we found." In the next breath she told everyone about the head.

"You uncovered a mouth?" The doctor sounded incredulous.

"I wish we could show it to you now, but the weather is acting up. Maybe by early evening we can do another dive. In the meantime, why don't you follow us to the cove where we spent the night on the beach? The site is right off the coast from there and a little east where we can eat before you leave for the port."

Everyone agreed it was a good idea. Alessandra raised the anchor and started the engine.

Once again they took off for the cove. While he stayed on the cruiser, Alessandra climbed out to chat with the others. They decided the storm wouldn't hit until evening, but it would be better not to go out diving again today.

"Are you staying here again tonight?"

"I'm not sure what our plans are, Gino, but we'll definitely be here tomorrow at nine to show you the dive site, unless the weather is worse."

Rini had checked ahead. There'd be a storm later. On impulse he picked up the chart and got out of the boat to show it to them. "In case we don't get together, I've marked the coordinates on here if you want to write them down."

Dr. Tozzi glanced at it and made notes on the pad in his pocket before handing it back to Rini. "Thanks."

"You're welcome."

The group prepared to leave. Nothing could have made Rini happier. So happy, in fact, that he handed Alessandra the chart, then helped push the other boats back in the water and waved everyone off.

Alessandra had to suppress a smile. Rini couldn't have been more helpful. How could any man measure up to the famous CEO who could scuba dive and read ocean charts with the best of them?

In a few more days, when he'd finished up business with her father, he'd fly off to Naples and his busy life that sent him all over the country. She had to remember he was only here in the south of Italy for a few more days. To think of him leaving was killing her.

If it turned out her parents agreed to let his company do some drilling, Rini would send out their experts. From time to time she'd see him coming and going from the castle. But for today and tomorrow, they would be together and it thrilled her heart.

She turned to him. "How would you like to do something fun?"

He cocked his dark head. "What kind of a ridiculous question is that to ask a man alone with a beautiful woman?"

"Just checking," she teased and got back in the boat with her heart thudding in her chest. "If you're game for a bumpy ride, I know a place where the food is divine. By boat it will take us about an hour and a half. When we get there we'll enjoy an early dinner and stay overnight."

"That good, hmm?"

"Yes."

"Only if you'll let me drive us. So far *you've* done all the work."

"I don't mind, but if that's what you want."

"It'll relieve my guilt."

"Over what?"

"I like to feel useful."

"You were amazingly useful when you pushed all the boats off the sand. You reminded me of Hercules."

His deep laughter resounded in the air.

"I'm not kidding. They would have had a terrible time in this wind without your help."

"If I impressed you, then it was worth the pain."

Her eyes scrutinized him from head to toe. "You did it so effortlessly, I doubt there's a sore muscle in your body."

He returned her gaze, sending the color flooding into her cheeks. "I guess it comes from both of us living in and out of the water."

She looked down. "Would you believe I still need to get out of my wet suit?"

"Do you need help?"

She felt the blush break out on her face. "I think I can handle it."

"While you do that I'll push us off and we'll get going."

Her chest fluttered as she hurried below deck to change and freshen up. After ascertaining that her parents had left her aunt's and had gone back to the castle, she joined Rini. He'd changed clothes and was seated in the captain's chair wearing his life preserver. "Tell me where to go."

Alessandra reached in the cubbyhole for her regular map and opened it, but the wind made it difficult to keep steady. "We're here. Keep following the coast past Metaponto, then we'll cut a diagonal and head straight for Taranto."

"That's where your aunt lives?"

"Yes. Our mother's titled family descends from the Duca di Taranto, although the title is now defunct, like my father's."

"Ah. It's all making sense." He put the map back and handed her a life preserver. "Sit across from me so we can talk."

She grinned. "Aye, aye, sir, but I don't think we'll be able to hear each other."

"As long as we're together, I don't care."

The man could read her mind. She sat on the banquette and stared out at a sea full of white caps. The moderate swells slowed them down, but she was having the time of her life. Since he hadn't vacationed in a year, Alessandra suspected he was happy, too, especially after he was the one to have picked the area where they'd made an underwater find. Every time he looked at her, his dark eyes burned with charged energy, melting her to the spot.

Outside Metaponto he stopped long enough to switch gas tanks. "I remember seeing Taranto's naval base and shipyards from the air."

"Then you know it's a big commercial city and port. Our Taranto relatives live in one of the eighteenth-century palazzi in the old town center. I've let my aunt know we're coming to see her. She broke her hip and has a nurse around the clock, but she loves visitors. Be warned she'll insist we eat dinner with her before we leave."

"I don't want to impose."

"She'll love it, Rini. Since you're a seafood lover, get ready to enjoy the most luscious roasted oysters you've ever eaten in your life. The cook prepares them in a special sauce followed by sea-bream-and-mussel soup. It's out of this world. Mother would steal her if she could."

He eyed her speculatively. "What's the other reason you're taking me there?"

You could never fool a man like Rini.

"She's mother's brilliant older sister by nine years and was married to a general who died two years ago. When Mamma was thirty, she almost died giving birth to me and Dea. Fulvia couldn't have children and was there to do everything. She won my father's devotion. As I told you earlier, her opinion goes a long way with both of them. I'd like you to tell her your business ideas for developing the property."

His features sobered. "Are you saying your mother doesn't approve?"

"I'm afraid not. Both of them were raised to be purists and believe that the former papal legacy should remain untouched."

"What about *your* opinion, Alessandra?"

She took a deep breath. "I've listened to my father and think your idea is an important one.

If a lot of oil is found, it *will* help the economy. But what's important is what Zia Fulvia has to say."

Those dark eyes searched hers. "Why are you trying to help me?"

A good question. "I believe in you *and* an even playing field."

"I'm humbled by your faith in me." He rubbed his jaw where the shadow of his beard was showing. She thought him irresistible. "Will I find her difficult?"

"Yes."

She loved the bark of laughter that came out of him.

"But you told me you like snags because they make life more exciting."

When he smiled, she felt herself falling toward him. "I did say that, didn't I? Let's go and get this over with. It couldn't be worse than a visit to the dentist."

Alessandra kept chuckling as the cruiser pounded the white water on its way to Taranto.

She'd never met anyone with a sense of humor like his. He was getting to her with every minute they spent together.

Due to the wind they made slow progress. It was after five when they passed through the outer and inner sea to pull into the private dock reserved for her aunt's family. Alessandra called for the limo that drove them to the Taranto palazzo in the old town.

"Tarantos have lived here for over four hundred years," she explained as they turned into the courtyard with its fountain supported by Taras, the son of Poseidon from Greek mythology. "You'll think you've entered a fabulous museum. Fulvia and Mamma were raised princesses and Fulvia still lives like one."

"She won't shudder at the sight of us fresh off the boat?"

At seventy-seven Fulvia was still all woman and would probably faint when she saw the gorgeous male Alessandra had brought with her.

"No. She's used to my showing up a mess after a day at sea."

Rini helped her out of the limo. "Lippo," she called to the older man who opened the ornate front door at the same time. *"Come stai?"*

"Bene, grazie, Alessandra."

"Please meet Signor Montanari."

"Piacere di conoscerla."

She looked at Rini. "Lippo and Liona are cousins. Our families couldn't live without them."

"Your families are close-knit in many ways," Rini murmured. "Does he have a cat, too?"

Alessandra chuckled. "He would, but my aunt has allergies."

"Signora Fulvia is in the drawing room, but she's tired since your parents left and is still off her food."

"We won't stay long."

"After you've spoken with her, dinner will be served in the small dining room."

"Grazie, Lippo."

Alessandra led Rini through hallways of marble floors and walls lined with gilt-framed portraits to her aunt's favorite room. Still a beauty, she sat in a wheel chair surrounded by the mementos of her deceased husband, who'd enjoyed a distinguished military career.

"*Buonasera*, Zia. I've missed you." She hugged her aunt. "I'm so sorry about your hip."

"A hazard of old age. Don't let it happen to you, *cara*." Her brown eyes flicked to Rini, assessing him with uncommon interest. No woman could help it. "Your fame as an engineer precedes you, Signor Montanari. Alessandra, why don't you see if your dinner is ready while I have a chat with him? Then I'll ask the nurse to take me to my room."

Her aunt had to be more miserable than she looked in order to get down to business this fast. "You poor thing. Please don't overdo it. I'll be right back." She shared a private glance with Rini before leaving the room. Though she felt the slightest bit apprehensive, he seemed perfectly at ease.

She didn't think anything could throw him. If he couldn't achieve his goal with her father, Alessandra knew he'd look elsewhere for oil because he was a man on a mission.

By nine thirty the bad weather had turned ugly. Rini felt the rain as he helped Alessandra into the limo and gave the driver instructions to return them to the private dock. Though she'd told him they could stay the night at the palazzo, the illuminating conversation with her aunt had turned him inside out and he'd wanted to leave.

Her aunt had told him something that had nothing to do with his business meetings with the count. She'd brought up an alarming personal issue that had a direct bearing on Alessandra and her sister. He needed to think long and hard about it for the good of the Caracciolo family before he shared it with Alessandra, *if he ever did.* The only solution was to kill his feelings for her. In order to do that, he needed to leave the castello and search for hydrocarbons elsewhere in the south.

"I'd rather get back to the cruiser. It will do fine while we wait out the storm." He imagined it would last all night.

"Well?" she asked with a smile after they'd gone below deck to the small room she used as an office. The rain pounded down outside. He stretched out in one of the chairs and extended his legs, crossing them at the ankles. Across from him sat the woman he considered the greatest beauty of the Taranto family bar none.

The humidity had curled the tips of her delightful hair. With her pink cheeks, she reminded him of one of the adorable cherub faces from Lecce. Her physical looks were a given. But what he found truly exquisite was her spirit—she had decided to give him a fighting chance to carry through with an idea, although it would never see the light of day now.

"I loved the tour of the palazzo and the meal was superb."

"It always is, but I'm talking about your chat with my aunt. How did it go? She was too tired to talk to me before she went to bed."

None of it was meant for Alessandra's ears. "I thought I was talking to a strong minded woman."

Laughter bubbled out of her. "She's tough all right."

Choosing his words carefully he said, "We talked pro and con. Her knowledge and directness impressed me before she asked to be excused to go to bed."

She eyed him curiously. "That's all you can tell me?"

Tight bands constricted his chest. "There isn't anything else."

"Oh, dear. It doesn't sound like it went well."

"I have no idea. But be assured I enjoyed meeting her and I'm indebted for your help. Since it's getting late, why don't you go on to bed? I've got business calls to make. Sleep well."

After they'd left her aunt's palazzo the night before, Alessandra couldn't believe the change in Rini. He seemed to have turned into a different man, and was aloof, preoccupied. What on earth had they talked about that made him so unapproachable?

She went down to her cabin and cried herself to sleep over the way he'd just shut her out. She'd been waiting for him to kiss her again, but it never happened. What he and her aunt had talked about had changed him in some way.

When Alessandra woke up the next morning, Rini was already at the wheel. The weather had to be better, otherwise the cruiser wouldn't be skimming across the water with such speed.

Why hadn't he knocked on her door to waken her? Anything to let her know he was aware of her.

She couldn't understand it and got out of bed

to dress. After making coffee in the galley, she went up on deck with her duffel bag in the hope he would be in a better frame of mind to talk to her.

But the second she saw the set jaw of that handsome face, she knew instinctively that now wasn't the right time. He was in no mood to confide in her. She walked over him. "I thought you might like this."

He eyed her briefly before taking the cup. "Thank you. You're an angel. As you can see, the storm has passed over. We'll have you home soon."

Home?

Her fear that something terrible was wrong had come to fruition. She frowned. "I thought we were going to dive. It's a great morning for it."

"I'd like to, but I'm afraid something came up while I made some business calls last night. I need to discuss them with your father. Please don't let that stop you from joining your group once you drop me off."

Diving was the last thing on her mind. She moved around and straightened the scuba equipment. They were almost to the island. Soon he eased the cruiser to the dock. When it was safe, she jumped out with her duffel bag and tied the ropes, leaving him to shut down the engine.

He joined her at the Land Rover. Their silent drive to the castle only took a minute, proof he was surprised she hadn't stayed in the boat before taking off again. Alessandra had the impression he couldn't wait to get away from her.

Sure enough, as soon as she'd parked the car, he reached for his backpack and got out. Alessandra followed him inside the foyer of the castle. He looked back at her. "I phoned your father earlier. He's waiting for me. Thank you for showing me your world. I loved every second of it."

So did I. Why are you acting like it's over? Rini—what's going on?

But he kept her in the dark. Without lingering, he walked toward her father's office.

With a heart that had fallen to the floor, she went up the staircase to shower and change into clean clothes. Her mother was probably in the day room so she hurried downstairs to talk to her. She would know what was going on with her father and Rini. This was a nightmare.

When she wasn't there, Alessandra went to the dining room and found it empty. "Hey, Alfredo. Are you looking for Liona?" She picked up the cat. On her way to the kitchen she heard the rotors of the helicopter. Someone must be arriving from the mainland. She kept on walking to the kitchen. No one was in there.

She lowered the cat to his food and water dishes, then she took off for her father's office. Maybe her mother was in there and she would find the three of them deep in conversation. After hesitating, she knocked on the door, unwilling to stay away any longer. "*Scusi*, Papà."

"Come in, *piccola*."

She found her father alone. "Where is everyone?"

"Your mother drove Liona to Metaponto for her dentist appointment." That explained why Alfredo looked lost.

"I—I thought Rini Montanari was still with you," she stammered.

He sat back in his leather chair. "He was here earlier to tell me that after thinking everything over, he decided that erecting oil derricks on our property would be a scab on the legacy Queen Joanna left to the family."

Those were the very words Alessandra had used. To hear her father say them brought inexpressible pain.

"He says he's off to search for another area to drill. After thanking both you and me profusely for our time and hospitality, he called for a helicopter and left."

Her legs started to buckle. She grabbed the first chair before she fell. "That's it? No other explanation?"

Her father smiled warmly. "Only to say that you discovered a large head while you were diving yesterday and he presumes it'll make you famous."

Except that Rini was the one with the inspiration to know where to dive.

"Oh—one more thing. He told me you're the most charming, lovely, intelligent woman he ever met and he understood why I wanted you to show him around. I could have told him that about you, but it's nice he discovered it for himself. As for the oil-drilling proposal, I have to admit I'm glad he withdrew it. Neither your mother or Fulvia were in favor of it."

"I know." A boulder had lodged in her throat.

"Fulvia phoned your mother early this morning. We were surprised to learn you'd taken him to see her. It made her very happy to see you while she's recovering."

But the visit had turned out to be devastating for Alessandra. Once again her world had been destroyed. This time she knew she'd never be able to put it back together.

Alessandra took a quick breath. "Since the

weather kept us from making another dive, I decided to pay her a visit. She was tired, but seems to be getting along fine."

"She was very impressed with Rinieri's honesty."

Honesty? What on earth did that mean?

Feeling ill, she got up from the chair. "I've been away from my work too long, so I'd better get busy or my editor will lose his patience. I'll be in the library if you need me." She hurried over to give him a kiss on the cheek before leaving the office.

When she reached her desk, she buried her face in her hands and sobbed. Several messages came in on her phone, all from Gino wanting to know if she would be joining them for the afternoon dive. None were from Rini.

Alessandra texted him that she couldn't make it, then left the castle in the Land Rover and drove to the mainland. After grabbing some food, she drove to the ridge where she'd taken Rini on that first day. The recent downpour had greened up the fields. She walked around, playing back their conversation in her head. Alessandra was convinced that the excuse he'd given her father not to drill wasn't the real reason he'd backed off.

Deeply troubled, she returned to the castle and got busy on the historical biography she was writing on Queen Joanna. But by Saturday morning she couldn't stand it any longer. Rini had been cruel not to have contacted her, if only to say goodbye. After what they'd shared scuba diving, she wasn't about to let him walk away until he'd listened to a few things she had to say.

If this was how he ended every relationship with a woman, no wonder he was still a bachelor. He'd been clever to abort their growing attraction before it burned out of control. Rini had been every bit as hungry for her as she'd been for him when they'd kissed. So why had he done this?

He'd been the one to pursue her, to want to scuba dive with her. There'd been no stopping him getting his way because she'd wanted to be with him so badly, too, and still did. So what had changed everything? Alessandra needed answers and she wasn't going to let him get away with it.

After telling her parents she'd be home late, she drove the Land Rover to Metaponto and took a commercial flight to Positano. Without her father's knowledge she'd looked up Rini's home address on his computer.

She could have gone to the Montanari office in Naples, but figured he'd be home on the weekend. If she walked in on him entertaining another woman, that was too bad. She needed answers.

Three hours later the limo she'd hired wound around the lush vegetation of his property. It stopped in front of a magnificent two-storied, ochre-colored villa, probably built at the turn of the century. Good heavens, the hilltop town above the Amalfi Coast was gorgeous beyond belief!

Alessandra marveled to know that Rini lived in this flower-filled paradise. The exterior was drenched in purple and red bougainvillea, robbing her of breath. So did the view of the sea from such a dizzying height.

A warm midafternoon sun shone down on her as she got out of the back. "Stay here, please," she said to the driver. She walked past several cars in the courtyard on her way to the front entrance. Alessandra hoped that meant Rini was home.

After using the bell pull, she waited for someone to answer and heard female voices inside. One said, "I'll get it, Bianca."

The moment the door opened, Alessandra knew she was looking at Rini's sister, who was a real blond beauty. Even though their coloring was different, the extraordinary family resemblance brought Rini to mind with a pang.

"*Buon pomeriggio, signorina.* Can I help you?" She'd answered the door in a bathing suit covered by a short lacy wrap.

Her heart was pounding too hard. "I hope so. I'm here to see Rini."

She studied Alessandra for a moment. "Aren't you the famous Diorucci model?"

CHAPTER FIVE

THIS WAS DÉJÀ VU all over again.

"That's my sister, Dea. I'm Alessandra Caracciolo."

"Well, you're both absolutely stunning."

"Thank you."

"I'm afraid my brother isn't here. I'm Valentina Laurito. Was he expecting you?"

"No." She swallowed hard. "I wanted to surprise him."

A mischievous smile broke the corners of his sister's mouth. "So did I. Bianca informed me he went fishing this morning and hasn't come back yet, but she's expecting him soon so I stayed."

Fishing...

While she took in the disappointing news,

an older woman appeared in the foyer carrying a darling blond baby boy, the image of his mother. She made the introductions. "Have you come far?"

"I flew in from Metaponto."

"That's quite a ways. Won't you come in and wait with me while I give my son a bottle? We're out by the swimming pool. Vito loves his Zio Rini and keeps waiting for him to walk out."

Alessandra knew the feeling well. "If you don't mind, I'd love to."

"Tell your driver to come back for you later."

She did the other woman's bidding, then walked through Rini's elegant villa. The patio furniture included tables, chairs and a large swing. Alessandra saw plastic toys in the water. Valentina took the baby from the housekeeper and settled him in his baby swing with a cover to shield his eyes.

"We have extra bathing suits if you'd like to change and take a dip."

"Thank you, but no."

"You might like it after your flight."

"It didn't take that long. Besides I get in plenty of swimming." Valentina was so easy to talk to, Alessandra needed to be careful what she said to her. Rini was a private person who wouldn't appreciate her getting too familiar with his family. Especially not after he'd left the castle permanently.

She found a lounge chair close to the swing to watch the darling baby. In a minute she heard rotors overhead and her pulse leaped. What would Rini think when he found her out here with his family? Maybe she shouldn't have come, but it was too late now because moments later her gaze darted to the tall, dark figure striding toward them from the other end of the pool wearing jeans and a T-shirt.

"There's your *zio*!" Valentina cried.

"Vito—" Rini called to him. The baby turned his head toward his uncle and lifted his arms.

That's when Rini saw her and his eyes narrowed. "Alessandra," he murmured.

Without missing a beat he came close and picked up the baby in his arms, kissing him. "What a surprise. Two visitors in one afternoon."

"Alessandra has flown here from Metaponto, but I can't persuade her to take a swim."

"That's because she scuba dives for the archaeological institute from Catania and probably enjoys a break from swimming."

Valentina's head swung toward her. "Rini's a master diver, too!"

"I know. Your brother was instrumental in helping me make a find the other day. I'm indebted to him."

"Rini," his sister virtually blurted with excitement. "You didn't tell me about that." Her eyes took in the two of them.

With enviable calm he explained, "While I was looking for new oil fields, I tagged along with Alessandra. She lives on an archaeological treasure."

"Zio Salvatore called me when he couldn't find you at the office. You know how upset he gets."

He played with Vito, avoiding Alessandra's eyes. "I'm back from Calabria now and got in touch with him."

"That's a relief. So how was fishing?"

"Good. Guido caught two trout with the lure I gave him. We ate them for lunch."

"Lucky you. I'm glad you came home when you did. Vito and I waited as long as we could, and now we've got to get back to Ravello. Giovanni will be wondering where we are." She turned to Alessandra. "It was so nice to meet you."

"You, too. Your little boy is wonderful."

"Thank you. I think so, too. I have another son, Ric, but he's with his birth mother today." She took the baby from her brother's arms and disappeared into the villa.

Alessandra was left alone with Rini. Her pulse raced at the way his eyes ignited as he studied her for a moment without saying anything.

She was glad she'd worn her white dress with the blue-and-green print, a favorite of hers. For once she'd knocked herself out trying to look beautiful for him. She'd even worn some eye makeup and had spent time on her hair.

"I think you know why I'm here," she said, answering the question he hadn't asked. "You didn't say goodbye." Her accusation hung in the air.

His hands went to his hips in a male gesture. "If you'll excuse me for a minute, I'll be right back."

"Promise?" she responded. He'd arrived dressed in outdoor gear with a navy crewneck shirt. With that hint of a dark beard on his jaw, she was almost overcome by his male virility. Alessandra had missed him so terribly, it hurt to look at him.

A nerve throbbed at the corner of his compelling mouth. "I swear it."

He left the patio on a run. She found a chair under the umbrella table and took in the sight of his own private Garden of Eden. So many species of flowers and trees astounded her, as everything looked perfect. All her life she'd lived in a castle surrounded by sand and water. Alessandra loved the isolation, but being here in Rini's home made her appreciate what she'd been missing.

The fragrance from the roses intoxicated her. She got up and walked around to smell the various varieties. Soon she heard footsteps behind her. When she turned, she discovered that the woman Valentina had introduced her to had come out on the terrace. She pushed a cart of food and drinks to the table. "Rinieri will be right out, *signorina*."

"*Grazie*, Bianca."

From the corner of her eye she saw a baby sandal left on one of the chairs. She started to retrieve it when Rini came out on the patio dressed in tan trousers and a silky black sport shirt. Freshly shaved, he looked and smelled fabulous.

Alessandra held up the sandal. "Your sister left this in her wake. I'm afraid her fast exit was my fault."

"You're wrong." He took the little sandal and put it on the table. "She couldn't wait to join her husband. They're crazy about each other." Rini held out a chair for her. "Sit down and we'll eat. One trout apiece wasn't enough for the appetite I've developed."

"I'm hungry, too. They only served snacks on the plane."

In a minute they filled up on shrimp salad with penne, dried tomatoes and slices of grilled eggplant that melted in her mouth. Rolls and lemonade with mint leaves made their meal a feast, but clearly Rini was a fish man.

Filled to the brim, she sat back in the chair. "I'm waiting for an explanation."

He wiped the corner of his mouth with a napkin before his gaze fell on her. "All along there's been something I should have told you about myself, but I never seemed to find the right time."

"What? That you lead a secret life? That you have a wife hidden somewhere?"

"Nothing like that. After the visit to your aunt's, I decided that I'd wasted enough of your family's time and thought it best to leave so you could get on with your dive."

She shook her head. "You're a man who was raised with good manners, so your excuse doesn't wash. Something happened during your private talk with my aunt that put you off your desire to drill on my family's property. I deserve to know the truth. It's only fair after providing you the opportunity to talk to her."

His eyes glittered. "You're treading on dangerous ground to ask for the truth."

Her hands gripped the sides of her chair. "Now I know I'm right. As you can see, I'm a grown woman and can take whatever you have to tell me."

Lines darkened his striking face. "I'm not so sure."

"Are you afraid I'm too fragile if you tell me a secret about yourself I don't want to hear?"

He eyed her somberly. "I have no desire to bring hurt to you."

Bring? Such a cryptic comment brought a pain to her stomach. "What do you mean? In what way?"

"You need to leave it alone, Alessandra."

Anger sparked her emotions. "I don't accept that."

"I'm afraid you're going to have to." He sounded so remote, her insides froze.

"In other words you really meant it to be goodbye the other day."

Rini leaned forward. "I'd hoped I'd made that clear when I left the island the other morning without letting you know my intentions."

The forbidding CEO of Montanari's had spoken.

Don't you dare break down in front of him.

She struggled for breath. "Don't worry. You've made me see the light. You and Francesco aren't that different after all. After he disappeared from my life, he sent his goodbye in a letter rather than face me. You flew off and left it to my father to do the honors. What is it about some attractive men? They seem to possess every quality except the one most vital."

A white ring appeared around his lips. She was pleased to see he wasn't completely impervious to her judgment of him. "Don't worry. Keep all your secrets! I'm leaving." She started to get up.

"No, Alessandra—you want the truth of everything, so I'll tell you. I never planned to, but since you've come all this way, I can't handle seeing you in this kind of pain. No one deserves an explanation more than you do."

"Go on."

"Where your aunt is concerned, we only talked business for a moment. The main thrust dealt with you."

"Me?"

Rini nodded slowly. "She loves you."

"I love her, too, but what does that have to do with anything?"

"She wanted clarification and asked to know what happened when I met Dea."

The moment he'd spoken, she stirred in the chair and averted her eyes. "I—I can't believe she brought up something that was none of her business." Her voice faltered. "Mother must have said something." After a long pause she said, "How uncomfortable that had to be for you."

"Not uncomfortable. I found it refreshing. You're a lot like her, you know. If I didn't know better, I'd think she was your mother."

Alessandra's head lifted. She blinked. "You're kidding—"

"Not at all. You and your aunt have a sense of fair play I admire very much. It's clear you both want the best for everyone. I told her nothing happened. Guido's father asked us to dance with the models he'd introduced us to. I had one dance with Dea, then she left. That was it. After my explanation, your aunt wanted to know my intentions toward you."

Alessandra shot out of the chair. "She had no right! I don't see how she could have asked you that when we hardly know each other!"

He stared up at her. "That's not true, Alessandra. Your aunt told me you've never taken a man to meet her before and what we had was something special. Naturally she's aware you've been showing me around for your father."

"So?"

"She realizes we would have learned a great deal about each other already."

"Well yes, but—"

"Her concern for both you and Dea is commendable," he interrupted. "So I had to be brutally honest and tell her that I didn't feel a connection to her. Since you and I met under the most innocent and extraordinary circumstances, she demanded to know if I felt a connection to you."

Alessandra paled.

"Don't you want to know what I said?"

"It's none of my business," she whispered.

"That's not an answer and you know it."

She turned away.

"I told her that my attraction to you was immediate and has been growing out of control." Her groan resounded in the air. "You feel it, too. I know you do. Out of loyalty to both her nieces, your aunt vetted me to make sure I wasn't using *you* to gain access to the legacy."

"That's absurd. I would never have thought that about you."

"But it's a mercenary world. She knew how hurt you were years ago and wanted to protect you."

"So you withdrew the proposal to prove to my family you had no ulterior motive? That's why you walked away from me?" Her voice rang out.

Instead of answering her, he reached for her

and drew her over to the swing, pulling her down on his lap. "Look at me, Alessandra."

She shook her head. "I'm afraid to."

"Because you know I want to kiss you. The other morning while we were on the sea floor uncovering the mouth on that head, I was reminded of you. When I kissed you on the boat, I was half out of my mind with desire. My motives *are* ulterior, but intensely personal."

"No, Rini. We mustn't. Not out here where Bianca can see us."

"*I* must, *bellissima*."

He curved his hand against the side of her face and turned it toward him. Obeying blind need, he covered her trembling mouth with his own. She tried to elude him, but he drove his kisses deeper and deeper until her little cry allowed him the access he craved. Maybe he was dreaming because she slowly began returning his kisses with a heart-stopping hunger that caused him to forget everything except the heavenly woman in his arms.

His hands roved over her back and shoulders while they gave and took pleasure from each other's mouths. He felt her fingers slide up his neck into his hair. Every touch fed the fire enveloping him.

"Alessandra," he moaned. "I can't get enough of you. Do you have any idea how much I want you?"

"I want you, too," she confessed, covering his face with kisses.

"During the dive I was dying to grasp your hips and pull you into a secret cave where we could make love for months on end."

"Our wet suits would have presented a problem."

"But not now." He eased her down on the swing, where he had the freedom to look at her to his heart's content while he kissed the living daylights out of her.

Rini had never known this kind of all-consuming desire before. The way she responded to him let him know something earthshaking had happened to her, too. She'd already had one love affair in her life, but it had been a long time ago. He was thankful it hadn't worked out because he was convinced she'd been reserved for him.

But what if she couldn't handle what he needed to tell her? He kissed her nose and eyelids. Before things went any further, she deserved to know the whole truth about him. Though terrified of her reaction, he couldn't stop now.

"You're the most divine creature this man has ever met. Since your aunt wanted to know my intentions toward you, it's only fair I tell you something about me first."

"You don't have to do this, Rini. You don't owe me anything. Please. I never dreamed my aunt would get personal with you like that."

"I'm glad she did. It woke me up to something I've been unwilling to face for years."

Her anxious eyes searched his. "What do you mean?"

"I've remained a bachelor for a reason."

"If you're allergic to marriage, you're not the

only man. Until my father met Mother, he decided he'd always be single."

"That hasn't been my problem. In truth I've never gotten to the point in my adult life when I needed to state my intentions. But with you, it has become necessary."

She lifted a hand to caress his jaw. "Why?"

He kissed her succulent lips. "You're not just any female I happen to have met. I'm not talking about the fact that you were born titled from both sides of your illustrious families. This is something that affects you as a woman. Don't you know you're head and shoulders above any woman I've ever known? Your pure honesty demands the same from me."

"Papà said my aunt was impressed with *your* honesty." She shivered. "What honesty is that? If your intention is to frighten me, you're doing a good job."

"*Frighten* might not be the best word." He sat up and got off the swing. "What I tell you will change the way you view me, but this has to come from me. I'll understand if you say it's been nice knowing you before you go your own way."

"For heaven sakes just tell me!"

Rini had angered her. This was going wrong. "From the time I could remember, I played soccer. By seventeen I was playing on a winning team with my friend Guido. On the day of the championship game, I got injured. At the hospital tests were done and I was told I was infertile. Over the years I've undergone tests, but the diagnosis is always the same…"

Her haunted eyes had fastened on him. She didn't move or cry out, but he saw pain break out on her face.

"Like anyone, I grew up thinking that one day I'd get married and have children. It was something I took for granted. Even after my first diagnosis, I didn't really believe it. I thought that surely in time the problem would go away and I'd be normal like everyone else. But every year I was tested, I was told that nothing had changed."

"I'm so sorry," she whispered, sounding agonized.

"So am I, Alessandra, because the diagnosis has impacted my life."

"So *that's* why you left me without saying goodbye? You thought I wouldn't be able to handle it?"

His lips thinned.

"Of course a woman wants babies with the man she marries. But there are other ways to have children."

"It's not the same. The other day when I was telling you about Valentina, you said you couldn't wait until you could have your own baby. It's a natural urge to want to procreate."

"Yes, but—"

"But nothing. I can't give any woman a baby, so I've been living my life with the reputation of being a dedicated bachelor. No one but my doctor, and now *you*, know I'm infertile."

"It happens to people, Rini. How tragic that you've let it rob you of the joy of life! It kills me that your fear has prevented you from settling down with a woman because you can't give her what you think she wants.

"I know you'd make a marvelous father, Rini. That's why there's adoption. Thousands of couples do it. For you to have lived your life since seventeen with such a dark cloud hanging over your head doesn't bear thinking about."

"You're very sweet, Alessandra, but you're not in my shoes." Her incredible reaction was all he could have hoped for and let him know her support would never be in question. His doctor had told him the right woman would be able to handle it.

But there was still something else to keep them apart. All of it stemmed from his conversation with her aunt and her implied warning. Even now he held back, thinking it was better that she believe his infertility presented the biggest problem for them.

Alessandra stared at him. "What you're saying is that you're going to let this stand in the way of our having a relationship. If you really mean that, then you need counseling before you deny yourself the greatest joy in life."

"Therapy won't help me," he responded bleakly. He rubbed the back of his neck. "Combined with the conversation I had with your aunt, a relationship with you won't work."

"We're back to my aunt again?"

"She told me some things in confidence I can't share. Don't be upset with her. It's because she loves you."

"Rini—" she cried out, aghast. But she'd felt him withdraw emotionally from her. It had been a huge mistake to fly here after all.

Alessandra pulled out her cell and called for the limo to return to his house. Once off the phone she got up and walked over to the table to drink the rest of her lemonade. "Please tell the cook the food was delicious. Now if you'll excuse me, I'm going outside to wait for my ride."

Rini moved faster than she did and caught up to her outside the front door of the villa. "Alessandra—"

"It's all right, Rini. Though your explanation wasn't the one I expected, I got my answer, so thank you. Please forgive me for barging in here uninvited. I give you my promise it will never happen again."

When the limo turned into the courtyard, she rushed to get in the backseat on her own. Rini was right there, but she refused to give him the satisfaction of meeting his eyes and closed the door herself. As the limo drove off, Rini's heart plummeted to his feet.

"Where do you wish to go, *signorina*?"

"The airport, *per favore*."

Alessandra didn't look back as they turned away.

No more looking back.

Just now she'd wanted to comfort him over his infertility, but she sensed he wouldn't have been willing to listen to her. For him to have revealed his agony to her had been huge for him. Now that he'd told her the truth, he'd backed away, certain that she—like any other woman—wouldn't see him as a complete man.

Was that image of being incomplete the reason for his meteoric rise in the business world? Had he worked day and night to compensate for what he saw as an inadequacy? She'd detected the love in his voice when he'd talked about his sister and her babies. Pain pierced her heart to realize that every time Rini eyed his nephew, he was reminded that he could never give a woman a child from his own body.

She'd seen the way he'd kissed and loved Valentina's baby. The man had been there for her throughout her pregnancy. Yet all that time, he'd been gutted by the knowledge that he'd never be able to look forward to having a baby from his own body. Her heart ached for him.

As for his conversation with her aunt, that was something else again. If he'd been sworn to secrecy, then she wouldn't be getting an explanation out of him. Alessandra could go to her aunt and demand to know the truth, but it wasn't her right.

On the flight back to Metaponto, she stared out the window of the plane. Rini Montanari had been an earthshaking interlude. But interlude was all he'd prepared for their association to be and became the operative word in her romance-less life.

Sunday evening the helicopter dipped lower over Ravello. Rini was late for his brother Carlo's birthday party, which Valentina and Giovanni were hosting.

For the last three weeks Rini had traveled to four areas of Calabria in Southern Italy, exploring the possibility of developing more oil sites. But he'd been in agony since Alessandra had left his villa and couldn't concentrate.

Nothing he'd visited turned out to be as promising as the land owned by the Caracciolo family. But he'd written that off. Unfortunately, blotting Alessandra from his heart was another matter entirely. With love in her eyes, she'd reacted to the news that he was infertile as if it was of no consequence to her. She'd assured him it didn't matter. The way she'd kissed him, as if he was her whole life, he'd believed her.

But her aunt's fear that a relationship with Alessandra might cause a permanent rift between the twins had prompted him to back away. Fulvia had told him how close the girls had been growing up, how much fun they'd had as children. But everything changed when Alessandra fell in love and then was betrayed by her sister and the man she'd thought she would marry.

The girls had finally gotten past it, but now they'd reached another impasse because Dea had met Rini first. Apparently she'd been devastated when he didn't want to date her. Hearing that Alessandra had been showing him around the property had upset her.

Though the situation was totally unfair, Fulvia had looked him in the eye and asked him if he wanted to be responsible for bringing on more pain between the two of them that might last. It was his decision to make.

In the end, Rini couldn't do it, so he'd had to let Alessandra go. All he could do was watch news clips on television about the discovery of the Temple of Hera beneath the waters off Basilicata in the Ionian.

Dr. Bruno Tozzi and his team had been given credit for the find and Alessandra's name had been mentioned. Every few days more information was being fed to the media about more discoveries of a courtyard and temple walls.

Rini was proud of Alessandra and the amazing work she was doing. Thanks to the coverage, he was able to keep track of her without having to make contact with her father. But having said goodbye to her had thrown him into a black void.

Once Rini arrived at the Laurito villa, he was besieged by family. He played with Carlo's daughter, then took turns enjoying the two baby boys. Giovanni chatted with him for a while, but it was Valentina who sequestered him in the sunroom just off the terrace. He couldn't get out of it.

"I thought you'd be bringing Alessandra with you. She's fabulous!"

"That's over."

"Why? I know you're in love with her."

His eyes closed tightly. "It can't work."

"Rini—are you saying she doesn't love you?"

He inhaled sharply. "She's never said the words."

"Have you?"

"It doesn't matter."

"Yes it *does*! Alessandra came to your house unannounced. I saw the look in her eyes when you walked out on the patio. If ever a woman had it bad…"

"There are things you don't know and I can't tell you. Don't make this any harder on me."

"Okay." She patted his arm. "I'll leave it alone. Keep your secrets and come on back out. Papà wants to talk to you and find out what new areas you've found for drilling."

"I wish I had better results to report."

Together they joined the others. Near midnight he flew back to his villa and did some laps in the swimming pool before going to bed. To his chagrin, sleep wouldn't come. He spent most of the night outside on a lounger.

Three weeks… If he didn't see Alessandra again soon, he'd go mad. But he had certain knowledge that bound him to stay away from her. Early Monday morning he put his emotional needs in the deep freeze and left for his office, prepared to announce some new sites for drilling that would please the board. He worked steadily until Thursday, when his secretary put through a call from his sister.

"Valentina?"

"Have you heard the news?" She sounded frantic.

His gut clenched. "What is it?"

"The seismic research facility in Malta registered a six-point-nine quake in the Ionian. The impact was felt all along the coast. It affected the diving site where Alessandra has been working with the institute."

Earthquake? He broke out in a cold sweat. *If anything happened to her, his life wouldn't be worth living.* To hell with what her aunt had told him. He needed to go to her and wouldn't let anything stop him.

"According to the news, apparently two or three divers were injured and transported to chambers at various hospitals on the coast. I found out the institute's oceanography boat docks at Crotone, so I'm sure some of the victims were taken there."

"I'm on my way. Bless you, Valentina."

He alerted his pilot and flew to the Naples airport, where he took the company jet to Crotone.

En route he phoned to make certain a rental car was waiting. Following that he made calls to the three hospitals in the town, but no one would give him information about the injured because he wasn't a relative. Other injuries over the southern area had been reported and hospitals all along the coast were filling.

Emergency vehicles and fire trucks filled the parking area of the first hospital. He made it to the ER and learned that one diver had been brought there. No one would give him information, but one of the ambulance crew helped him out by telling him they'd transported a male diver here.

Thanking him, Rini drove to the next hospital. Again it was the wrong one. He made the rounds until he reached the last hospital. When he spotted Bruno Tozzi in the waiting room, he knew Alessandra had to be here. Avoiding conversation with him, Rini walked through the hospital to the director's office. He'd do whatever it took to be granted permission to see her.

* * *

"I'm fine," Alessandra assured her parents after she'd spent six hours in the chamber.

"Are you in pain?"

"No, not at all. The doctor told me I have a light case of the bends."

"Dr. Tozzi wants to see you."

"He worries about all the team, but I'm not up for visitors. Tell him I promise to call him tomorrow when I'm feeling better."

"All right. We'll find him out in the reception area and be back in two hours. The doctor said you'll be here overnight. We'll stay with you and drive you home in the morning. Try to rest in the meantime. Love you." They kissed her before slipping from the room.

No sooner had they gone than the door opened again. It was probably the nurse coming in to check her vital signs. When she saw who entered the room, her heart fluttered dangerously fast.

"*Rini*—what are you doing here?" After three

weeks of not seeing him, the sight of his tall, well-honed body wearing a navy blue business suit was too much to handle in her weakened state.

"When I heard what happened, I couldn't stay away."

She turned on her side, trying to hide from him. "Did you talk to my parents?"

"They don't know I'm here."

Her breath caught. "You shouldn't have come. We've said all there is to say."

"I had to be sure you were going to recover," he said, his voice throbbing.

Tears stung her eyes, but she refused to let him see them. "I don't see how you found out where I was."

"A simple deduction after Valentina phoned me with the news about the epicenter of the quake."

She sighed. "How did you get past the desk? No one is allowed in here."

"I have my ways. Alessandra, you could have

died out there. The doctor said you lost consciousness. It could have been fatal. Do you
have any idea what I've been going through
thinking I might have lost you?"

"Maybe now you know how I felt when you
let me leave Positano and I knew it was over
with you." A bitter little cry escaped her lips.
"My parents will be taking me home in the
morning. The only reason I can imagine you're
being here is because of your guilt.

"What a surprise I'm going to survive! Surely
it's a relief to you. That way you don't have to
tell me what you've been holding back. It would
only add to your guilt."

"Alessandra—" His mournful voice reached
that vulnerable place inside her before he'd
come around the side of the bed. She felt him
cup her face with his hand. "*Grazie a dio* you're
alive and safe."

She kept her eyes tightly closed. "I admit I'm
happy about it, too."

His fingers toyed with her hair, sending fingers of delight through her exhausted body. "I once came down with a case of decompression sickness and know how it feels."

"One of the hazards when you're having fun."

"You don't need to pretend with me. I know you've had a fright and need sleep. Do you mind if I stay here with you for a little while?" He leaned down and kissed her lips. It felt like the touch of fire.

"The doctor won't like it, but that's up to you."

Peering at him through slits, she watched him draw a chair to the side of the bed next to her. He looked like a man with the weight of the world on his powerful shoulders. She needed him to go away and never come back, but she couldn't find the words.

In a minute a nurse came in to bring another bag for her IV. She checked Alessandra's vitals and left without saying a word to him. The man could get away with murder. "What did you do to get permission?"

"I told the administrator that Montanari Engineering would make a generous donation to the hospital if they'd let me in to see you."

There was no one like him, her heart cried out. "Rini Montanari. That was a naughty thing to do."

"It worked. That's all that mattered to me. To find you alive means everything. These last three weeks without you have been a hell I never want to live through again," he admitted, his voice breaking.

His pain was tangible. "Now you'll have to make good on your offer and work all hours of the day and night to recoup the loss."

"It'll be worth it since the hospital helped save your life. You're the most precious thing in my world. I love you, *bellissima*," he said in the huskiest voice she'd ever heard. "Now go to sleep and don't worry about anything."

When Alessandra woke up in the middle of the night, she decided she'd been dreaming that Rini had come to visit her. Had he really said he loved her? There was no sign of him. The night nurse came in and helped her to the rest-room, then walked her back to bed.

CHAPTER SIX

THE NEXT MORNING Alessandra awakened to find her parents in the room. They'd brought her a fresh change of jeans and a soft top, which she slipped into. At 11:00 a.m. the doctor discharged her with the proviso that she rest, stay hydrated and do no diving for at least fourteen days.

It felt good to be wheeled outside to her parents' limo. They made her comfortable before driving her back to the castle. Yet not at any time had they or the medical staff mentioned that Rini Montanari had been a visitor.

She'd really experienced a whopper of a dream to imagine he'd left his office to fly to Crotone in order to find out if she was all right. Alessandra was terrified it would take years, maybe a lifetime, to get over him. But what if she couldn't? The ache in her heart had grown acute.

Instead of going upstairs, she told her mom she wanted to stay in the day room and curled up on the couch under a quilt to watch television. Supplied with water and nuts, she didn't lack for the creature comforts. Alfredo wandered in and jumped up on her lap. He supplied the love she craved.

"Alessandra?" She lifted her head to her mother. "Are you up for company?"

"If it's anyone from the diving group, could you tell them I need a few days?"

"It's Rinieri Montanari."

She reeled in place.

"He said he visited you at the hospital, but the nurse put something in your IV and you fell asleep. He's anxious to know how you are."

Rini *had* been there!

She hadn't dreamed it after all and couldn't believe it. Thrilled, yet tortured by what her mother had told her, she couldn't concentrate on anything else. "I—I look terrible."

"That would be impossible," her mother assured her, "but if you want me to send him away, I will."

"No—but don't tell him to come in yet. Could you hand me my purse? It's over on the credenza."

Her mother did her bidding. Alessandra's hand trembled as she brushed through her hair and applied a coat of lipstick.

"Ready?"

Alessandra nodded. While she waited, she checked her phone to find a dozen texts from friends, one of them from Bruno, who wanted to know how soon she'd be back. Fulvia had sent her love and condolences. She wanted a good talk with her when she was feeling better.

Alessandra's editor was thankful she was all right and told her not to feel pressured about delivering the book. He hadn't given her a deadline. But there was no message from Dea, the one person Alessandra wanted to talk to. The pit grew in her stomach as she realized her own sister hadn't tried to contact her. Why?

"You don't look like you've been sick," said the deep, familiar male voice she was dying to hear.

She looked up at the sinfully gorgeous man. "You're right. I'm a fraud."

Rini walked over to her. He'd dressed in jeans and a pullover sweater in slate blue. Combined with the soap he used in the shower to assail her, his presence had put her senses on overload. He reached down to scratch behind the cat's ears. "You have the right instincts, Alfredo. I'd trade places with you if I could."

In the next instant he leaned down and pressed a warm kiss to her mouth. "Welcome back to the land of the living. Your doctor told me you lost consciousness down there."

"Only for a moment. My buddy Gino knew exactly what to do. It all happened so fast."

"We can be thankful the divers with the institute are experts." He stood there looking down at her with an intense expression.

She squirmed. "Rini?" Her voice shook. "Why are you here?"

"Though I had my reasons, I treated you badly when I left here the first time without saying goodbye. My behavior was worse when you flew to Positano to see me and I wouldn't explain myself. I thought I was doing the right thing both times, but your accident has changed the way I feel about everything.

"I love you and I've never said that to another woman in my life. Almost losing you has made me realize I could no longer let my reason stand in the way of being with you, so I'm back to find out if you'd be willing to start over again with me."

While she sat there in shock, Liona wheeled in a tea cart laden with a meal for them. "If Alfredo is bothering you, I'll take him out."

"Oh, no. I love him right here. Thanks, Liona."

After she left, Rini got up and served both of

them a plate of food and her favorite iced tea. His gaze found hers. While they ate he said, "Life has given both of us a second chance. What I'd like to do is invite you to my villa for a week where we can spend real time together."

Alessandra couldn't believe what she was hearing. She said the first thing that came into her head. "Can you take a vacation?"

"Of course. I want to get to know you without work or interruptions getting in the way. The nice thing about being CEO is that I can arrange it when I want. The doctor told me you shouldn't dive for at least two more weeks. You've shown me your world. Now it's time I showed you mine."

She smiled. "Like fishing?"

"Only if you'd want to."

"Rini, I adore the outdoors. Hiking, camping, all of it."

"The mountains are beautiful this time of year. Could you talk to your editor and ask for an extension to turn in your book?"

"He already told me to take all the time I need."

If only Rini knew she loved him so much she felt like she could move mountains for him, but she was afraid. "When the week is over, *then* what? Will you consider you've done everything possible to obtain my forgiveness?

"Will we say goodbye like sensible people who've enjoyed their interlude together but knew it had to come to an end? You'll go your way because you can't offer me any more than what you've already done? I'll go mine?"

His jaw hardened. "Why don't we stop worrying about the future and just take things one day at a time? I need help because I've never done anything like this before."

She took a deep breath, surprised to hear the vulnerability in his voice. "Like what?"

"Invite a woman I care about to stay at my house."

"I've never done anything like it, either." Talk about needing help...

"The doctor told me you need rest and that you shouldn't fly until tomorrow. So if I leave you now, will you think about my invitation? I'll call you in the morning. If you decide you want to come, I'll arrange to pick you up in the limo and we'll fly in the company jet to Positano." He stood up.

"Where will you be in the meantime?"

"At the airport in Metaponto. I'm working in my office on the jet and will stay in the bedroom overnight. I'll give you until ten a.m. to get in touch with me. If I don't hear from you by then, I'll be flying back to Naples."

She knew he meant it. This was it.

"If you'll give me your phone, I'll program my number for you."

Alessandra handed it to him. "Rini, whatever my answer is, I promise to call you."

Lines marred his arresting features. "I can't ask for more than that." He put the phone on the table. "You need rest now. Take care of yourself, *adorata.*"

The second he disappeared from the day room she wanted to call him back and tell him she'd go with him right now. But she needed to keep her wits about her. The decision to spend a week with him would change her life forever.

She kissed the cat's head. "Who am I kidding, Alfredo? My life changed beyond recognition the day he approached me in the foyer."

He said they'd take things a day at a time. She had no choice but to do what he wanted because at this point she knew she couldn't live without him. If it was only for a week, so be it. The man was so complicated it was driving her crazy. Somewhere in the mix, Rini's inability to give a woman a child had stunted his vision of life. She wanted to help him explore the world of adoption so he'd realize he could know total fulfillment.

With her heart ready to burst from the joy his invitation had brought her, she lay down and didn't awaken until hours later, when she heard her parents' muffled voices talking about her sleeping her life away.

Alessandra sat up, disturbing Alfredo, who jumped to the floor. "What time is it?"

"Time for you to be in bed. Let's get you upstairs."

Later when her mother tucked her in bed she told her about Rini's invitation. "I want to accept it, but I'm afraid."

"Don't let what Francesco did keep you from reaching out for your own happiness."

If her mother only knew this had nothing to do with Francesco. But at least she had her parents' blessing.

Liona brought her breakfast at eight, after which Alessandra pressed the button programmed to phone Rini.

"Am I going to hear what I want to hear?" he answered in that deep voice. She thought she heard a trace of nervousness and loved him for it.

"Maybe, unless you've had a change of heart during the night."

"Alessandra—don't keep me in suspense."

Her mouth had gone dry. "I want to come, but I need time to pack."

"How much?"

She chuckled. "Do we have to leave by ten?"

"I don't care when we leave today as long as you're with me."

"Then can we say noon?"

"I'll be at the castle at twelve and we'll eat on the plane during the flight."

"It sounds wonderful. Ciao, Rini."

After ringing off, she hurried around her room to get ready for her trip. She needed to pack everything under the sun. Normally she traveled light, but not this time. Besides sportswear for their outdoor activities, her plan was to bring a few new bikinis and evening dresses that would knock his socks off.

She turned on her radio to some light rock music. The cat wandered in her room and probably thought she was out of her mind as she danced around filling her two suitcases.

"Alfredo? You should see his gorgeous villa."

"Whose villa would that be?" asked a familiar female voice.

Alessandra spun around. "Dea!" After being caught off guard, she hurried over to her sister and hugged her. "I didn't know you were coming." With Rini coming for her, she couldn't believe the bad timing.

"Evidently not. Papà told me about your accident so I came home to see how you are. I thought you'd still be in bed recovering. I never expected to find you flying around your room having a conversation with the cat. What's all the packing for?"

"I—I'm going on a trip," she said, her voice faltering.

"I gathered as much." Dea's eyes looked at the bags on the bed. "I do believe you've emptied your drawers and closets. Are you finally giving Bruno Tozzi a chance? He's been after you for over a year."

"Not Bruno. I've never been interested in him that way. Actually I'm going to be a guest at Rini Montanari's villa." She'd had no choice but to tell her sister the truth.

At the mention of his name, any goodwill Alessandra had hoped could be resurrected between her and Dea on this visit had vanished. Her sister paled. Rini really had hurt her by not asking her out again. "Are you talking about the one in Naples or Positano?"

Of course her sister would know all about Rini. She'd danced with him on his friend's yacht. "I assume Positano."

"Is this because you showed him around the property for Papà?"

"Dea? Please sit down so we can talk." Alessandra closed the lids on her bags. "He'd been scuba diving with me. It's a sport we have in common. When he heard about the earthquake, he flew down. Yesterday he came by the castle to invite me to stay with him for a week."

"You mean he hasn't been here all month?"

"No. He's been gone for weeks on business. I was surprised to see him again." So surprised she'd thought she'd been dreaming when he came to her hospital room.

Dea's eyes followed her around while she packed her cosmetics. "I was shocked to learn he had business with Papà in the first place."

"Let's agree it was a shock all the way around." Alessandra was so uncomfortable she could hardly bear it.

Her sister studied her for a minute. "Be honest with me. Are you going with him because of what happened with Francesco?"

"No, Dea—not at all! How can you even think that?" Alessandra cried. "Whatever happened is long since buried in the past." She sank down on the end of the bed. "What do you want me to say?"

"Have you fallen for him?"

"I care for him very much."

"As much as you did Francesco?"

"You can't compare relationships. Francesco was my first boyfriend. I was young. As you reminded me, he ended up being a loser."

"Don't you know why I told you that?"

Alessandra frowned. "What do you mean?"

"He wasn't interested in me. Within a day of his arriving in Rome, he was chatting up another model."

"Oh, Dea—I didn't know that."

"I thought Mother would have said something. I'm telling you this to warn you about Rinieri Montanari."

Alessandra didn't want to hear it.

"On the yacht, his best friend's father, Leonides Rossano, confided in me that Rinieri was Italy's most eligible bachelor—as if my best friend, Daphne, and I didn't already know it. I read between the lines and deduced he'd been a player for years. Alessandra—he might

end up breaking your heart after he gets what
he wants from Papà."

"You're wrong about that, Dea. He doesn't
want anything from him," she replied, defend-
ing Rini. "He withdrew his proposal weeks ago
and has been looking elsewhere for oil in the
southern part of Italy."

"I didn't know that. Sorry." Dea stood up, but
Alessandra could tell the revelation had shaken
her. "How soon is he coming for you?"

"At noon."

She looked at her watch. "It's almost that time
now. I don't want to be around when he arrives,
so I'll join the parents while you get the rest of
your packing done. I'm glad you're recovered.
Even gladder that I wasn't the one under the
water when the quake struck."

A rush of warmth propelled Alessandra toward her sister. She put her arms around her
again. "Thank you for coming. You don't know
how much it means to me."

Dea hugged her back. "You've always been

the brave one." She kissed her cheek before disappearing from the bedroom. Alfredo followed her out the door.

The brave one?

An hour later those words were still chasing around in Alessandra's psyche as Rini helped her out of the limo to board the Montanari jet.

Once they'd attained cruising speed, his steward served them an incredible lunch of lobster pasta with *sfogliatelle* for dessert. The shell shaped pastry had a divine ricotta filling with cinnamon. The wonderful flavor was beyond description.

They sat in the club area by the windows. His dark eyes never left hers. "I'm glad to see a smile. When I picked you up, you seemed preoccupied. For a moment I was afraid you still didn't feel well enough to come. We could have left tomorrow."

"I'm fine, Rini, but I have to admit I'm still a little tired."

"After what you experienced, that's understandable. When we get to the villa, you can rest all you want."

She looked out the window, wishing she felt the same excitement he'd engendered in her when she'd told him she would accept his invitation. But Dea's unannounced arrival had taken her by surprise. Though touched that she'd come to see her after her scuba-diving accident, her sister's questions about Rini had put a damper on this trip.

He was doing everything in his power to make her comfortable and had no idea Dea had been at the castle when he'd picked her up. She didn't want him to know, let alone tell him what her sister had said. Dea hadn't been unkind. Alessandra had been grateful for that, but she couldn't help feeling that her sister was suffering in some way.

Alessandra remembered how she'd felt when she'd first talked to Rini in the castle foyer. The immediate, overpowering attraction she'd felt for him had to be swallowed in the knowledge that he'd already been with Dea. She'd wondered then if she'd ever be able to get over him.

Yet today, her sister had to handle the news that Rini wanted to be with Alessandra enough to invite her to his home. If Dea had felt the same overwhelming attraction to him that night on the yacht, then who knew how long it would take her to get over Rini, especially if he ended up being in Alessandra's future. The thought haunted her.

"I think you really are tired." Rini got out of his seat and adjusted hers so she could lie back. "Our flight won't last long, then we'll put you to bed in the guest bedroom until you're feeling your old self."

"Thank you." But she no longer knew who her old self was. Life had taken on new meaning since she'd met him.

Something was wrong beyond Alessandra's fatigue. Rini had sensed it the moment she'd met him outside the castle doors with her suitcases.

He'd expected to be invited in to speak to her parents, but she'd whisked them away as if she was in a great hurry. Rini hadn't questioned her about it. In time he'd get answers. They had a whole week. Today was only the beginning.

Once the jet touched down, the helicopter flew them to the villa. He carried her luggage while she made her way along the path that led to the back patio. She looked over her shoulder at him. "You truly do live in a garden. At home I smell the sea air. Here, I'm assailed by the most heavenly scents."

"After living in Naples with the occasional scent of sulfur from Vesuvius in the air, I chose this flower-filled mountaintop on purpose. Follow me through the house. Your room faces on the pool. You can walk out the French doors at any time and take a swim. Come on. Let's get you in bed."

He saw her eyes widen in appreciation when they entered the bedroom off the hallway. "It's a lovely room. Those blue hydrangeas on the coffee table take my breath."

"I'm glad you like them. Go ahead and freshen up. I'll be back in a minute." He put her cases down and left to get her a bottle of water from the kitchen. Rini had given Bianca the next three days off so he could be alone with Alessandra and wait on her himself.

When he returned, he found her sitting on the side of the bed still dressed in white culottes with a sharp front crease. She'd layered them with a multicolored blue silk top and looked so sensational, he couldn't take his eyes off her.

"I thought I'd find you under the covers. This is for you." He put the water on the bedside table before opening the shutters to let in the early evening light from the pool area.

She smiled up at him, but it lacked the joie de vivre he'd seen while they'd been out diving. "I'll sleep tonight. Now that I'm in your world again—but only because you invited me this time—I want to talk to you. Please sit down."

He sat in one of the upholstered chairs by the coffee table.

"Where's Bianca?"

"On a short holiday."

"So it's just you and me?" He heard a slight tremor in her voice.

He frowned. "Are you worried about being here alone with me?"

"Of course not." She got up from the bed and walked over to smell the flowers. "Can we have a frank talk? You said you wanted to start over again. I want that, too, but I need to understand you better."

Rini sat forward with his hands clasped between his legs. "Would I have brought you here if I didn't want the same thing? We've got all the time in the world. Go ahead. Ask me anything."

She darted him a curious glance. "You say that, but I wonder if you really mean it."

"Where's this doubt coming from?"

"I don't know exactly. Tell me about what happened when you first met Dea. Being twins, she and I have shared a unique past. Sometimes it has been eerie."

"In what way?"

"It's hard to explain, but there are times when even though we're two people, we think as one."

Rini got to his feet. "I've heard that happens to twins. But what does that have to do with me?"

"I'm not sure and am only feeling my way," she cried softly before turning away from him.

He put his hands on her shoulders and pulled her against him. "You sound frightened," he whispered into her fragrant hair.

"I am."

"Of what? Of me? Tell me." He shook her gently.

"I've been going over the conversation that my aunt had with you about me and Dea. You told her that you felt no connection with Dea, but it was different with me." Alessandra turned around in his arms. "But it doesn't provide all the answers."

"What more do you want?"

Her eyes searched his. "Will you bear with me a little longer and tell me your feelings when you realized I wasn't Dea?"

His hands slid to her face. "After I left your father's office and went back to my hotel in Metaponto that first night, I couldn't get you off my mind. Make no mistake. It was *you* I was thinking about. From a distance you had Dea's superficial features, the same features that had drawn me on the yacht. But the second you said you weren't Dea, I realized my mistake.

"You looked so adorable standing there in your shorter hair and man's shirt that didn't cover up your bikini. Tanned, no makeup, bare-legged, full of energy, duffel bag in hand. I thought, I've got to get to know this exciting woman! I told your aunt I felt a connection so powerful with you, I couldn't wait to get back to the castle the next morning to see you again."

He felt Alessandra's anxiety before she eased out of his arms. "Thank you for being so honest with me." She was shivering.

"Now that I have, do you want to tell me what's going on in your mind?"

"After I entered the castle, I heard a voice call out *signorina*. You'll think I'm out of my mind, but when I saw you walk toward me, it was like seeing the prince who'd haunted my dreams come to life before my very eyes. I felt your imprint on me before you said a word.

"But the second you started talking, I realized you thought I was Dea and my dream was crushed to grist. She'd had a history with you. She'd been there first. I'd never experienced such envy in my life. I've heard of love at first sight, but I never imagined it would happen to me. My pain that she'd met you first was too excruciating to bear."

Her eyes glistened with unshed tears. "Until I learned the truth of your relationship with Dea during our drive, I'd been forced to keep my feelings bottled up and pretend nothing was wrong in front of my father."

Her words shook Rini. *"Adorata."* He reached for her, but she took another step back. "I haven't finished. There's something else you need to hear."

Rini couldn't take much more and attempted to get his emotions under control. "What is it?"

"When Dea and I were little girls, we had many of the same likes and dislikes that in some cases baffled everyone. One of the things we had in common was to talk about the princes we would marry one day. We played our own form of house with a miniature castle and all the characters Papà had made for us.

"Our mother and aunt gave us beautiful clothes to dress our dolls. Dea always had the most glamorous and stupendous outfits because they knew how much she loved fashion. I was given a fabulous boat that would sail me and my prince around the castle and the world."

The lump was growing in Rini's throat.

"We played for hours about living in the castle all our lives and being happy forever with our princely husbands and children. In our case it wasn't pure fiction considering the lives of our titled parents and heritage."

"Alessandra—"

"Let me finish," she interrupted. "You were there when she first laid eyes on you. You saw what I can't see. Rini, I'm convinced that when Dea met you on the yacht, she had the same experience I did. She saw you sitting there and knew you were the prince of her dreams. It was one of those times we were both the same person. By the expression on your face, I can tell I'm right."

He closed his eyes tightly for a minute. *Incredibile!* This talk with Alessandra answered the questions that had lingered in his mind about Dea. In view of what he'd just learned, the way she'd linked her arms behind his head and the ardent kiss she'd given him when they'd stopped dancing as if she'd been claiming him for her own made a strange kind of sense. Her actions had borne out Alessandra's theory.

Guido had acted nonchalant about it, but Rini had seen the glint of envy in his friend's eyes. That was the only time he'd ever known him to show a side of emotion that surprised him. But Rini couldn't be that cruel to Dea or Alessandra by telling her what Dea had done that night to show her attraction to him. It had to be a secret he would take to the grave.

His head reared. "What you're saying is, Dea is now the one devastated."

"Maybe."

"Then we're back to where we were before. If your guilt is going to keep you from enjoying this vacation with me, then I'll fly you back home in the morning."

"No, Rini—that isn't what I want. I just needed to have this conversation with you."

"But it doesn't solve anything, does it?"

"I guess I want you to tell me what we should do."

"If you mean that, then I suggest we table

our concerns and enjoy our vacation. We'll just have to hope that time and work will help Dea get over whatever disappointment she's feeling." But that wasn't going to be easy since he still hadn't forgotten the conversation with her aunt. He'd been burdened by it. "As for you and me, I'd hoped to take us on an overnight hike tomorrow."

"You know I'd love that."

"Then we'll pick you up a lightweight backpack and sleeping bag in the morning." She nodded with a smile. "How are you feeling now?"

"Much better. I'm getting hungry and know you are. Why don't we go out to dinner someplace in Positano."

"I've been anxious to show it to you. If you're ready, we can go now."

CHAPTER SEVEN

As Rini helped Alessandra into the black BMW parked in front, he squeezed her waist and kissed the side of her neck. When he reached for her hand and held on, her heart pounded with anticipation of the night to come. He started the car and they wound through the lush greenery toward the town center. She could see the twinkle of lights from the fabulous villas half hidden behind cypress trees and palms.

The interior of the car smelled of the soap he used in the shower. She was so in love with him it was impossible to hide it from him. If she didn't put Dea out of her mind, she could ruin this incredible time for them.

"Whoa. We're right on the edge of the cliff."

Rini flashed her a smile and parked the car

along the side of the narrow road. "We've arrived at my favorite place. You'll love the view from here." She could hear soft rock music as he helped her out. They walked up the rock steps lined with flowers growing out of the vegetation to the little restaurant perched high up. The view from the terrace, where a band was playing, opened to the sea below between two mountain sides.

She gasped and clung to him. "That's a steep drop."

"Kind of like dropping eighty feet with you in our own private world." Trust him to remind her. "Come on, *bellissima*."

He put his arm around her shoulders and guided her to an empty, candlelit table. The romantic ambience made her feel feverish. Rini seated her and asked for wine from the waiter who recognized him. "Will you trust me to order for you?"

"If you'll trust my cooking when we eat along the trail tomorrow evening."

"I can hardly wait." After the waiter walked away, Rini reached for her hand and pulled her onto the small dance floor, where another couple was dancing.

"There's no room for anyone else."

"That's the whole idea," he whispered before biting her earlobe gently. They danced in place, sending her body temperature skyrocketing. "If you knew the dreams I've had about holding you like this. Tonight there's no wet suit to separate us."

She chuckled. "I noticed."

"I never want to be separated from you," he admitted in a husky voice and crushed her to him. Alessandra closed her eyes and rocked in place with him. Never sounded like forever. Was it really possible? But that question led to the troubling question about Dea still hanging over her head, shooting more pain to her heart. So it was better not to think, just relish this night under the stars with Rini.

"I could stay this way indefinitely," she murmured, "but I can see our food has arrived. Let's get you fed."

"How lucky am I to be with a woman who understands me." He walked her back to their table and they plunged into an exquisite meal of octopus on creamed potatoes and prawns, followed by vegetables and *carpaccio* of swordfish with a dessert of *salame de chocolat.*

"If we keep eating like this, I'll have to buy me a larger wet suit," she quipped.

His dark eyes glinted with amusement. "We'll hike it off tomorrow. For now you need to get home to bed. It's been a long day for you."

"I have to admit bed will feel good tonight."

"I knew it." He paid the bill and ushered her out of the restaurant. "Careful as we go down the stairs. Hold on to me."

She didn't need his urging as she clung to him. He walked her to the car, keeping her hugged against his side. Before he opened the door, he lowered his head to kiss her. She'd been dying for it. The passion he aroused in her was so powerful, she almost fainted. Someone in a car driving by let out a wolf whistle, causing her to blush in embarrassment. Rini only chuckled and opened the door so she could hide inside.

"Sorry about that," he murmured as they drove back to his villa.

"No, you're not."

"Would you believe me if I told you I couldn't help myself?"

Yes, if his desire for her was half as great as hers for him. She rested her head against the back of the seat. "This has been a wonderful night. I rarely drink wine and am afraid I drank too much."

His hand reached out to give her thigh a squeeze, sending rivulets of desire through her body. "One glass?"

"Already you're a corrupting influence on me."

Male laughter rang inside the confines of the car. "Didn't you know you've become my addiction? You'd better lock your door tonight."

She rolled her head in his direction. "I trust you, Rini."

"Maybe you shouldn't."

"If I didn't, I wouldn't be going camping with you. Where are you going to take me?"

"Along the footpath of the gods."

"Did you just make that up?"

"No. It's the name of a trail formed by man years ago along the Amalfi Coast. In my opinion it's one of the most striking panoramas of this world. You'll know what I mean when we get going. We'll follow it part of the way through gorges and precipices, then veer inland into the mountains."

"You've given me goose bumps."

"When you uncovered the mouth on that head, it raised the hairs on the back of my neck."

She eyed him with longing. "I can't believe how you just happened to know where to dive."

"Pure selfishness. I wanted you to myself." He pulled into the courtyard and escorted her inside the villa to her bedroom. Putting his hands on her shoulders he said, "Tonight was the perfect way to start our vacation. I'll see you in the morning and we'll get going whenever you're ready. Sleep well."

He gave her a brief kiss before exiting the room. It was a good thing. If he'd lingered, she wouldn't have let him leave.

Before she went to bed, she hung up a few things in the closet, then checked her phone. Her mother had texted her to find out how she was feeling since her hospital stay. There was no mention of Dea, who was probably still there. Alessandra texted her back, telling her she felt fine and that they were going hiking tomorrow. She sent her love to her parents. But when she climbed under the covers, her heart ached for Dea, whom she knew was in deep pain.

The ringing of the house phone at the side of the bed awakened Alessandra the next morning. She checked her watch. Seven thirty a.m. He was a morning man who loved fish. Little by little she was learning those precious things about him. With a smile she reached for the phone. "*Buongiorno*, Rini."

"Hot coffee is waiting for you in the kitchen when you're ready, but there's no hurry."

The excitement in his voice was contagious. She swung her legs over the side of the bed. "If I told you I couldn't make it until noon, you know you'd have a heart attack."

"Please don't tell me that."

"You'll have to be patient with me," she teased. "Ciao."

She hung up the receiver and raced around the room getting ready, once she'd taken a shower. After diving into her suitcases, she pulled on jeans, a T-shirt and hiking boots. She packed a cloth bag she'd brought in her suitcase. Quickly she filled it with extra clothes, socks, a hoodie, a flashlight, matches, cosmetics and a brush— all the little things needed for their hike. She'd attach it to the backpack they were going to buy her.

When she hurried through his elegant home

to the kitchen, she discovered she'd only taken eight minutes to get ready. Not bad considering the gorgeous male drinking coffee had assumed she would keep him waiting for hours.

The look of surprise on his handsome face was so comical, she thought he would drop his mug. Alessandra grinned. "Got ya."

His eyes blazed with intensity. In the next breath he wrapped her in his arms and whirled her around. "I figured five more minutes and I was charging in to get you."

"Now I wish I'd waited."

A bark of laughter escaped his throat before he kissed her fiercely. He didn't let her go until she struggled for breath. "I've made breakfast. Go ahead and eat while I take your bag out to the car with the food I've packed."

"You made food for our hike? I could have helped."

"Bianca always has my favorite meat and cheese pies on hand. We'll pack some to take with us."

"I'm salivating already."

She reached for a ham roll and grapes. After swallowing coffee, she hurried out to the car. Rini locked up the house and they left for the town to pick her up a backpacking frame. He knew exactly what he wanted for her and soon they were on their way to the outskirts of Positano, where he parked the car in an area reserved for hikers.

Rini was a master at assembling all the gear, which included a tent, fishing gear plus all the other things they'd brought. "How does that feel?" he asked after helping her adjust the straps. "Is it lopsided?"

"It's perfect and the day is absolutely glorious."

Through her sunglasses she stared at the striking male specimen standing before her wearing his own pack. He carried the bulk of their equipment as if it was nothing and smiled back at her through his sunglasses. "Get ready to be astounded by the sights."

"After you, Captain."

They were off. She followed him along a well-worn path for about a mile. Before she knew it they'd come to a section with a thousand-foot dropoff and no railing. "Rini," she squealed in awe.

"We're at the top of the cliff. You'll notice that people live up here and use this path coming and going."

"It's a miracle. Unbelievable." They continued walking and ran into farms and terraces that grew fruits and vegetables.

"Some people come here for a hike and decide to live here in one of the little houses on these mountains."

"I can see why. It's so peaceful up here, unconnected to anything else."

"You should be here during a storm. The clouds drift in from the sea and literally collide with the cliffs."

"The view from this spot is breathtaking. That water is so blue, I have to take a picture." She pulled the phone out of her pocket and insisted he get in it. They took turns so he could capture her, then they trudged on.

Alessandra really did feel she was walking on the footpath of the gods. One of them was right in front of her. He took such wonderful care of her every step of the way, she felt cherished.

They stopped at noon to eat lunch under a tree, then made a turn into the interior. Rini was an encyclopedia on the flora and fauna, let alone the history of the region governed by Byzantine rule from the third century when Amalfi was a trading post.

He took her past gorges and caves until they came to a mountain stream. "How are you at fly fishing?"

"I've only trolled for fish in the sea. You'll have to teach me."

"You're going to love it. Let's have a snack, then I'll set up our fishing poles and I'll show you how to cast."

It felt good to sit down and relax for a little

while. He told her to look in his tackle box and see what kind of fly she'd like to use.

"Do they all work here?"

"Most of them. Look for a gray spider fly."

Alessandra rummaged around until she found one of that color. "This?" She held it up.

"That's it. I'll attach it and we'll walk down to the edge of the water to catch our dinner."

She watched him put her fly on the line before he chose a spot. "Show me how to cast."

He demonstrated five or six times so she could get the hang of it. "Okay. I think I'm ready to try." But it wasn't as easy as he made a look. She hit too low, too high and was too jerky. On her last cast she put the fly rod too far back and her line was snagged by a shrub. "Oh, no!"

Rini didn't laugh outright, but she knew he had to be chuckling as she scrambled up the side of the ravine to retrieve the fly. She made several attempts to no avail. "Help! I can't get it out!" He joined her and carefully extricated it from the prickly bush. "You're so good at this I bet you've never done that."

"You have no idea the mistakes I've made," he confessed after pressing a hungry kiss to her mouth. "Come on. Let's try it again."

"I'm embarrassed and want to watch you fish for a while."

He reached for his pole and aimed for a spot near a rock where the water pooled in the stream. On his third attempt to catch something at the same place, she saw a little fish grab his fly and he reeled it in.

"That was poetry in motion, Rini. I'll never be able to do that."

"Keep at it and you'll become an expert like you are at everything else." He got out his fish knife and removed the hook before throwing the fish back in the stream.

"Why did you do that?"

His eyes lit on her. "It was too small. Maybe he has a big brother or sister swimming around. Now it's your turn to try again."

She reached for her pole. "I'll aim for the same place you did." This time she threw it so hard, her pole landed in the water. *"Diavolo!"* she cried and jumped into the fast moving stream to catch it. But her boot tripped on a rock and she felt flat on her face. Her pole was carried farther downstream and got stuck around a bunch of rocks.

Like lightning Rini was there to help her up. By now they were knee-deep in the water. She lifted her head, not knowing whether to laugh or cry. His body was shaking with laughter, but being polite, he held it back. She loved him so much, she couldn't stay angry and started to laugh.

"Apologies for the slip."

His smile enveloped her. "Which one?"

"Both!" She broke free of his arms and made her way carefully downstream to recover her pole. "Ooh—a big trout just swam past me. I wish I could have grabbed it!"

Rini's deep male laughter poured out of him in waves. He moved toward her.

"No, no. I can make it back to shore myself. You're probably thinking, is this the scuba diver?" To her horror, the moment she said the words she slipped on a moss-covered rock and fell on her face, making another big splash.

When she stood up sputtering, there was Rini taking a picture of her. "That's not fair." Alessandra made a face. "This is ridiculous." She raised her rod and stomped out of the water, flinging herself down on a grassy spot. "Don't you dare laugh again."

Rini raised his hands. "I wouldn't dream of it. I was hoping we could hike farther to a small lake, but under the circumstances we'll camp here. I'll set up the tent so you can change out of your wet clothes."

"I'm all right. Let's keep going. Maybe I'll have better luck at the lake. I'll just troll for a fish by walking through the water and trailing my line."

One dark brow lifted above eyes that were dancing in amusement. "You're sure?"

"Let's go." She put on her backpack, deciding to carry her pole as is.

Rini started out first. All along the way she heard him chuckling, but he never turned around. A half hour later they dropped into a dark green gorge. With night falling fast, she was reminded of a primeval forest. The water from the stream emptied into a silvery narrow lake maybe a soccer field long. "It's shaped like a fat eel!"

"Spoken like a scuba diver. My father always thought it looked like a cigar."

"What about your brother?"

"A long blimp."

She laughed. "And you?"

"The Veil Nebula."

Alessandra blinked. "You love astronomy?" He nodded. "Did you ever consider becoming an astronomer?"

"No. The universe is too far away. With engineering I can get my hands on something once I design it."

"You like the tactile."

He nodded. "We'll set up camp here."

"I love this spot."

"Tomorrow we'll explore the other end of the lake. The water trickles down to become a waterfall and cascades to the sea."

"I wish we didn't have to wait."

His gaze trapped hers. "You know the old saying. All good things come to those who wait."

"But I don't want to. Aren't I awful?"

"Later tonight I'll tell you what I think."

His words filled with promise almost caused her legs to buckle. In seconds he'd found them a grassy area and pulled out the blue-and-white two-man tent. She helped him erect it. They worked along in harmony. Finally she was able to go inside and change into warm gray sweats and tennis shoes. All her clothes needed to be dried outside, including her boots.

While he built a small campfire, she laid their

sleeping bags side by side. The whole time Alessandra worked, she feared he could hear her heart thudding through the walls of the tent. Tonight they'd be sleeping together. This was the kind of heaven she never imagined could happen to her.

The light from the flames flickered, revealing his tantalizing male features. He'd thrown on a tan crewneck sweater over his jeans. His beautiful olive skin and dark coloring had been bequeathed by his Neapolitan ancestry. She could feast her eyes on him all night.

He watched her approach. "Come and sit down. I've made coffee to go with our pies."

"You're wonderful." She kissed his jaw before making a place next to him. "I'm sorry I couldn't contribute anything for our dinner. I'll do better another time."

"I'm counting on it," he murmured.

Her pulse raced as she sipped her coffee from the plastic mug. "Did your mother camp with you when you came out here?"

"Many times. Valentina, too. It's dark in this part of the mountains. She would bring her hand telescope and pass it around. I remember the hours she taught us about the constellations. Then she and Papà would slip into their tent and leave the three of us to enjoy the wonders of the universe. When I grew old enough, I understood they sneaked away to enjoy the wonder of each other."

"Oh, I know all about that." Alessandra chuckled. "Our family went on expeditions to Sicily. One time at the Valley of the Temples, we'd set up our camp. I thought we'd explore that first night while there was still light. But our parents told us to run along and enjoy ourselves.

"My sister and I eyed each other. We could always amuse each other. But it was another one of those times when we were both thinking exactly the same thing. You could say that night contributed to our enlightenment. I never looked at my parents the same way again."

Rini ate another pie. "I can relate." He let the fire burn down.

She sat cross-legged in front of it. "You've never told me where you went to school."

"University of Naples, then MIT in Cambridge, Massachusetts."

"You didn't meet a special woman during those years?"

He swallowed the rest of his coffee. "Yes, but I had a goal to finish my education and didn't let anything get in the way."

"Still, you know what I mean."

"She didn't matter enough to distract me from my agenda since I knew I couldn't give her a baby."

"I'm glad it didn't work out. Otherwise I wouldn't be with you now."

Rini stirred and got to his feet. "I want to continue this conversation, but would rather do it in the tent. Give me a minute to put out the fire." While he went over to the stream half a dozen times for water to douse the flames, Alessandra put the food away, then found her flashlight and took a trip behind a fat bush.

She kept the light on for Rini. Once she'd removed her tennis shoes, she entered the tent and lay down inside one of bags. Before long he joined her having exchanged his sweater and jeans for a dark blue sweatshirt and pants. His dashing smile took her breath. "I'm having the most fun I've ever had in my life."

"So am I."

He zipped up the tent flaps and opened the little screened window for air. Then he stretched out on top of his sleeping bag and turned toward her. "Do you mind if we keep the light on for a little while? I want to look at you while we talk."

She rolled on her side to face him. "I love looking at you, but you already know that."

"Alessandra?" He reached for her hand and kissed the palm. "Though I want to make love to you and never stop, I can't wait any longer to tell you what's on my mind first."

"What is it?"

"I'm helplessly in love with you, *adorata*, and want to marry you."

A cry escaped her throat. "Rini—"

"That couldn't be news to you." He sat up to face her. "I fell in love with you that first day. You weren't the only one who had a surreal experience."

Joy permeated her body. "I hoped you felt that way, but I hardly dared to dream I would ever hear those words."

"I've been afraid to say them because of the burden it puts on you."

She raised up on one elbow. "What burden? If you're talking about the fact that you can't give me babies, we've already had this conversation. It doesn't matter."

He shook his head. "Of course it does. But putting the reality of adoption aside, I'm talking about something else that I should have discussed with you weeks ago."

Weeks?

With that word Alessandra got a sinking feeling in the pit of her stomach and sat up. "This has to do with my aunt, doesn't it?"

Lines marred his features, letting her know she was right, and her frustration grew. "Instead of going diving that morning, you drove us back to the castle because you said you had business with Papà."

"I did," he muttered.

"That's interesting. When I came down to the office later to find you, he told me you'd gone. I heard the helicopter. According to him you were no longer interested in drilling for oil on our property. As a footnote he said you thanked both of us profusely for our time." Her voice quivered, but she couldn't stop it. "I thought I was in the middle of a nightmare."

Rini was quiet so long, she couldn't stand it. "What went on with my aunt behind closed doors that caused you to leave without even having the decency to say goodbye to me in person? If what happened was so terrible, why didn't you tell me immediately?"

"I held back because I didn't want to betray a confidence that could bring pain."

"You've said that before. To whom?" she demanded.

He stared her down. "Everyone involved."

"I don't understand." Her tears had started. He brushed them away with his thumbs.

"My feelings for you ran so deep, I was afraid to spend another moment with you. The only thing to do was get away and never see you again."

She shuddered. "Don't you know how cruel that was to me? I'd fallen hopelessly in love with you and you knew it."

"Listen to me." He grasped both her hands. "I slipped away because I thought it was the best thing to do considering that I never intended to see you again."

Alessandra couldn't take much more. "Then why did you come back?"

"You know the answer to that. When I heard about the earthquake and knew your diving team had been affected, I came close to having a coronary. Nothing could have kept me away, not even my reason for leaving you the way I did in the first place."

"The accident didn't turn out to be that serious."

"It could have been deadly," he argued. "Don't you know *you* were the most important person in my life? To think of losing you was so terrifying, I flew out of my office and left for Crotone. I had to search for you at two other hospitals before I found you. The moment I saw you again and your doctor told me you would recover, I realized I couldn't walk away from you a second time."

"Even if what you're about to tell me will hurt everyone?" Her question rang inside the tent.

"Yes. I have to risk it because I've just asked you to be my wife. But I was premature and don't want your answer until you've heard the whole truth from me."

A groan came out of her. "How long are you

going to make me wait? Please just tell me what it is and let it be the end of all the secrets."

The sick look on her face devastated Rini, but she needed to hear everything. He drank part of his bottle of water first, then screwed the top back on. "Did you know that Dea flew to Taranto to see your aunt the morning after being on the yacht?"

A delicate frown marred her features. "That's news to me. I thought she told you she had some fashion shows that kept her in Naples."

Rini nodded. "That's what she told me. Does your sister have a special bond with your aunt?"

"Yes. Many times over the years she's gone to stay with her. My aunt took care of her after she was born so Mamma could have a break from two children at once. I usually spent time with our mother. I adore my aunt, but I'm pretty sure Dea developed a deep attachment to Zia Fulvia that has lasted. Our aunt is very glamorous and exciting. Naturally it meant the world to her since she couldn't have children.

"I've always appreciated that Dea and I were raised to be individuals. Neither Mamma or Fulvia played up our twin status. We were never dressed alike or put in the same classes at school. They wanted us to be able to express ourselves in our own way and have our own friends. Dea gravitated to Fulvia."

"Yet interestingly enough, in some ways you're more like your aunt than she is."

"You told me that before." She took a ragged breath. "You still haven't told me why Dea went to see her."

After listening to the explanation of Alessandra's background, Rini was beginning to understand a great deal. "Your sister wanted to talk to her about me."

A haunted look crept into her lovely face. "I'm surprised my aunt would reveal something that private to you."

"So was I, until she explained herself. I'm convinced that what she told me was motivated out of pure love for both you and Dea."

Alessandra lowered her head. "What did she do? Ask you to stop seeing me?"

"No. That's exactly what she didn't do. For the first few minutes she told me a story about a wonderful, brilliant girl who fell in love with a chef from Catania named Francesco and got her heart broken. Fulvia feared this girl would never get over it and never be able to forgive her sister, whom she'd always felt was more beautiful and loveable than herself. To Fulvia's great surprise and joy, this girl *did* get over her heartache. She seized life to the fullest without blaming her sister for anything."

"What?" Alessandra's head flew back in shock.

"That's right," Rini murmured. "Then she told me a story about another exciting, bright girl who fell for an engineer named Rinieri Montanari. He represented her prince incarnate, but she discovered he didn't feel the same way about her and she wanted to die."

Alessandra's chin trembled. "Oh, Rini..."

"*Oh, Rini* is right. Your aunt asked me to think carefully before I took another step. She feared Dea might not be as strong and courageous in battling her heartache as was the scholarly twin she'd always envied."

"Dea envied me?"

The shock on her face was priceless and told him this was a woman without guile. "She left me with a question and a warning before she went up to bed. Her exact words were, 'Is the recent love you feel for Alessandra greater than the lifetime love between twin sisters? Whatever you decide, you'll have to live with the consequences forever.'"

Rini didn't know how she'd respond after telling her the truth, but he hadn't expected her to turn away from him and sob into her pillow. "*Cara—*" He lay down next to her with his arm around her shoulders. She convulsed so much, all he could do was hold her and kiss her cheeks and hair until the tears eventually subsided. "Talk to me, *bellissima*."

After a long time she turned over, her face blotchy from crying. "The warning she gave you felt like someone just walked over my grave."

"Why do you say that?"

"Because when I found out you'd met Dea first, I determined to put you out of my mind. Nothing was worth coming between my twin and me since we'll be sisters forever. I was taken by surprise when Papà asked me to drive you around the property. Much as I wanted to be with you, I knew it would be taking a great risk. Fulvia's words have just confirmed my worst fears."

Gutted by her response, Rini shut off the flashlight and lay down on his back. "I'm sure your aunt didn't want me to reveal our conversation to you, but my world changed after your accident and I had to tell you."

"I'm thankful you did. I know she spoke to you out of love for Dea and me." He heard Alessandra's heavy sigh. "It took a lot of courage on your part to tell me and I admire you for keeping quiet about it for as long as you have in order to protect Dea."

"What worries me now is where you want to go from here."

"I don't know, Rini. In the morning I'll have an answer. Thank you for the greatest day I've ever known. *Buonanotte.*"

He heard the rustle of her sleeping bag. She'd turned away from him physically and emotionally. Unable to lie this close to her without reaching for her, he stood up and went outside to walk around. A three-quarter moon lit up the night sky. He didn't need a flashlight or a fire to see the forested landscape. The lake shone a mystic silver.

She's not going to marry you, Montanari. I can feel it in my bones.

Rini felt like he was burning up with fever. The cool night air brought some relief. He eventually planted himself beneath the trunk of a pine tree close to the tent so he could keep an eye on her. Several times he nodded off, but was wide awake at six craving coffee.

After making it, he heated it on the ultralight stove. Once he'd downed a cup, he walked over to the stream. Though he cast his line half a dozen times, nothing was biting yet. Maybe it was an omen to prepare him for what was to come.

He could have kept the secret he'd shared with her aunt, but wouldn't have been able to live with it long. Alessandra's tearful breakdown proved to him he'd done the right thing telling her. But it was possible he'd written the death sentence on a future life together with her.

Near eight o'clock she stepped outside the tent with a false smile, dressed in another pair of jeans and a white pullover. One by one she produced their sleeping bags, all rolled up and snug in their cases. He didn't have to hear a word from her to know their vacation had come to an end.

Her eyes darted to his. "*Buongiorno*, Rini. I

detected coffee. It smells so much better out in the forest, don't you think?"

Without saying anything he poured her a cup and handed it to her.

"Grazie." She eyed his pole. "I heard your line snaking in the air. Evidently you didn't have any luck fishing this morning or you'd be cooking our breakfast."

Rini had all the chitchat he could take. "Why don't you just tell me what I already know," he groaned.

This morning she was dry-eyed. "Papà once said that Zia Fulvia was the wisest woman he'd ever known. After what we talked about last night, I'm convinced of it. I'm honored by your marriage proposal, Rini. No thrill will ever equal it. But even if I'll love you to my dying breath, I don't want to see you again. I'm ready to hike back to the car whenever you say."

CHAPTER EIGHT

A WEEK AFTER returning to the castle, Alessandra realized she couldn't go on in this state of limbo. Even if she could dive again, she didn't want to. The thought of working on her book was out of the question. She unpacked all the gorgeous clothes she hadn't worn and put them away. Rini was on her mind night and day.

Though her parents didn't question her when she returned home having cut her vacation short, she knew they wanted to. But her father didn't probe and she was thankful for that. Her aunt came to stay for a few days to enjoy a change of scene. Soon she'd be able to get around without the wheelchair.

Fulvia was as warm and loving as always, giving nothing away about her private conversation with Rini. They did some puzzles as a family and Alessandra learned that Dea was back in Rome after another sensational show in Florence attended by some VIPs in the television industry.

But talking about Dea had been like pressing on a thorn until she was bleeding all over the place. The day after her aunt flew back to Taranto, Alessandra told her parents she was taking the Land Rover to visit friends in Metaponto and wouldn't be back until evening.

She gave Alfredo a kiss on the head before leaving the castle. "I don't like lying, but this is one time no one can know where I'm really going."

Once she reached the airport, she boarded a flight for Rome. The plane landed at noon. After hailing a taxi, she asked the driver to take her to the elegant apartment complex in the heart of the city where Dea had been living for the last year. The five-hundred-year-old street where it was located was a warren of fabulous shops near the Pantheon and the Piazza Navona.

When Alessandra approached the desk manager, he called her Signorina Loti. "You've mistaken me for her. Would you please ring her room? I'm her twin sister and have flown a long way to see her."

The middle-aged man did a double take. "*Scusi, signorina.* It's astonishing how much you two look alike. Except for the hair... I suppose in this case it will be all right to let you in."

"Thank you, *signor.* You're very kind."

Dea had a fabulous apartment on the third floor. Fulvia had come to Rome to help her furnish it in a lavish style. After she'd been let in and freshened up, she went out again and left a note for the manager to give Dea when she came in from work.

Four hours later she returned to the apartment building having eaten and done a little book shopping while she thought about what she was going to say to her sister.

"Signorina? Your sister came in ten minutes ago."

"Grazie."

Her heart pounding with anxiety, Alessandra took the lift and knocked on her apartment door. Dea opened it looking gorgeous in harem pants and a filmy short-sleeved top of aqua. "This is a surprise."

"For me, too."

"Come in."

They hugged before she walked into the living room. She put down her sacks and turned to her sister. "Forgive me for not letting you know I was coming. I didn't decide until this morning."

"No problem. I thought you were still on vacation in Positano."

She shook her head. "I returned early."

Dea eyed her critically. "What happened to change things?"

"That's what I want to talk to you about. Do you have time, or do you have other plans?"

"Not tonight. If you want juice or fruit, it's in the fridge."

"Thanks, but I've already eaten.

Her sister sank down on the sofa. "Go ahead. What's on your mind that has brought you all the way here?"

"The last time we saw each other, you asked me if I was seeing Rini because of what happened with Francesco."

"And you told me no. Why are we talking about this?"

She sucked in her breath. "Because I'm tired of ignoring the elephant in the room and I have a feeling you're sick of it, too."

Dea averted her eyes. It told Alessandra her sister knew exactly what she was driving at.

Tears sprang into Alessandra's eyes. "I'm going to tell you something I've never admitted to you before. From the time we were little, I looked up to you as my big sister."

"Three minutes hardly qualifies me for that title."

"It did for me because you came out first and no one let me forget it. You were beautiful and made friends easily. Everything you did was elegant and perfect. As I grew older, I felt more gawky and insecure around you. By our teens guys flocked around you. I'm ashamed to admit I was so jealous of you."

She had to be getting through to her sister because Dea lifted her head and stared at her in disbelief. "You…were jealous of me?"

"Oh, yes. When Francesco followed you to Rome, I didn't want to believe it, but deep down I wasn't surprised. I'd seen the way he'd looked at you. He never looked at me like that."

"I'm sorry, Alessandra," she cried.

"No, no. Don't be. You didn't do anything to attract him. You don't have to. It always happens because you're you. For a long time after that I lived in denial about it. Finally I realized I needed to grow up and face the fact that I could never be like you. It meant I had to work on myself."

"But you're perfect just the way you are!"

It was Alessandra's turn to stare at her sister in wonder.

"It's true. All my life I've been the one jealous of you. You're beautiful without even trying and you're smart. You write books and do all these amazing things with the underwater archaeological society. I've envied your love of adventure and hated it that I have so many stupid fears."

Alessandra shook her head. "I had no idea."

"We're a mess," Dea muttered. "Since it's truth time, want to tell me why you're not still with Rinieri? He's the most gorgeous hunk of manliness I ever saw."

"I agree," she said quietly. "But I wish I hadn't met him."

"That's the biggest whopper of a lie you've ever told."

"*Dea—*"

"It's true. You're mad about him. So what are you doing here with me?"

"Y-you know why," she stuttered.

"Because I had a giant-sized crush on him first? That's true, but he wasn't enamored of me no matter how hard I tried to entice him. It killed me that he didn't want to see me again. I even told Zia Fulvia."

Alessandra swallowed hard to hear the admission she already knew about.

"She laughed and said, 'Dea Caracciolo—do you want to conquer every man you meet? What would you do with all of them? It's not natural!'"

Alessandra's laughter joined Dea's.

"She gave me a simple piece of advice that made sense. 'When the true prince of your dreams comes along, it'll work. Until then, dry your tears and do your thing you do better than anyone other woman in the country.'"

"Fulvia's wonderful."

"She is. So are you, and Rini Montanari is absolutely smitten with you. Otherwise he wouldn't have invited you to his villa for a whole week. The famous bachelor has fallen to his knees. If you don't snap him up, then you're a fool."

"You mean it?"

"Oh, come here." Dea reached out and hugged her hard. "I have something else to tell you that should make you happy."

"What?"

"I made a play for him. He didn't bite."

"What kind?"

"On the yacht, I kissed *him* good-night right on the mouth."

"Good grief!"

"Don't worry. He didn't kiss me back and turned me down when I asked him to go out to dinner with me the next night. Only an honorable man would do that. You're a very lucky woman and I'll welcome him into our family with open arms."

"I love you, Dea, and want only the best for you."

"I know that, and I love you, too."

"Let's never let anything come between us again."

"Never."

"We're sisters forever."

Forever.

"Now let's go on a shopping spree and find you an outfit that will deliver the coup de grâce the moment Rini sees you. Why not show up at his office and dazzle everyone in sight?"

"I only want to dazzle *him.*"

"Then let's do it!"

The Montanari office complex dominated a portion of a city block in the downtown business center of Naples. At four in the afternoon, Alessandra was met by whistles and stares as she stepped out of the limo in her Jimmy Choo heels. She was wearing the designer dress Dea had picked out for her. It cost a fortune but she didn't care because she felt transformed in it.

The solid off-white pullover dress with long sleeves had a row of trendy buttons up the side

from the tulip-styled hem to the neck. Around
her shoulders she wore a flowing ivory-and-tan
print scarf that matched the tan-and-ivory lace
of her shoes.

Her hair glinted with streaks of gold among
the brunette. She wore new lipstick in a deep
pink with a soft blush on her high cheek-bones
and a touch of eye shadow Dea said brought
out her eyes. She'd never been so decked out.
Her sister said she'd never looked more beautiful. Alessandra felt like she was moving in a
fantastic dream.

His office building was like a small city,
forcing her to pass through security before she
could approach the bank of elevators. Her pride
in his accomplishments made her throat swell
with emotion as she rode one of them to the
thirty-sixth floor, where his headquarters was
located. She approached the secretary in the
main reception area.

"I'm here to see Signor Montanari."

The attractive, thirtyish-looking woman looked up, then blinked. "You're Dea!"

Alessandra smiled, not minding it at all. "No, but you're close. I'm her sister."

"Do you model, too?"

"No. I scuba dive."

"Oh." Her blue eyes rounded. "Which Montanari did you wish to see?"

"Rinieri."

"I'm sorry, but the CEO is in a board meeting and can't be disturbed. If you'd like, I'll make an appointment for you."

At least he was here and not out of town. "Thank you, but no. I'll wait until he comes out."

"It might be several hours."

"I don't mind." *I'd wait forever for him.*

She sat down on one of the love seats with her ivory clutch bag in hand. Twenty minutes later she saw an attractive, dark-haired man who bore a superficial resemblance to Rini walk into the

reception area and hand something to the secretary. His brother? A cousin?

The secretary must have said something to
him because he turned in Alessandra's direction. Their eyes met before he walked over to
her. "I understand you're here to see Rinieri?"

"Yes, but he didn't know I was coming. I
wanted to surprise him."

The flattering male admiration in his eyes
made her efforts to look beautiful worth it.
"He's going to be surprised all right. I'm going
back in to the meeting. I'll let him know someone is out here waiting for him, but I won't give
you away."

Her heart fluttered in her chest. *"Grazie."*

"Prego."

Twelve men sat at the oblong conference table.
Rini's Zio Salvatore scowled at him from a few
seats down on the right. "I think we're moving
too fast. Look what's happened in Greece!"

"If we don't strike now, someone else will."

Rini was tired of the deadlock. Tonight he'd reached the end of his rope. He was ready to take off for places unknown to forget his pain. Guido had tried to talk to him, but Rini was in such a dark place, he wasn't fit company for anyone. Something had to change or his life wasn't worth living.

"My son's right," Rini's father said. "With this uncertain economy, we have to take advantage of these opportunities while we can."

While everyone offered an opinion, Carlo came back in the room. His brother's brows lifted, a signal that he wanted to talk to him about something. It would have to wait until they'd resolved the issue before the board.

"Let's take a vote," his cousin Piero said.

"We're not ready yet!" This from Rini's great uncle Niccolo.

The arguing went on another fifteen minutes. Rini received a text on his phone. Just so you know, Octavia said you have one more appointment before you leave tonight. The person is waiting in reception.

Since when? Rini didn't have the time or inclination to do any more business once he left this room, but he nodded in acknowledgement to Carlo, who sat at the other end of the table. When five more minutes hadn't yielded a consensus, Rini brought the meeting to a close.

"It's late. We'll reconvene on Monday and take a vote then." Salvatore couldn't have been more pleased that no action had been taken yet. He came from the old school, unable to abide the kind of progress Rini felt the company should be making.

After slipping out a side door into his private office, Rini rang Octavia. "Send in the person who's been waiting. Since they're infringing on my weekend, tell them I can only give them one minute. My helicopter is waiting."

"Yes, sir."

While he leaned over his desk long enough

to sign a pile of letters ready to be mailed, he heard a knock on the door.

"Come in."

"Signor Montanari? Please forgive me for barging in without an appointment, but this is a matter of life and death."

He knew that voice and spun around, convinced he was dreaming.

"Cat got your tongue?"

The vision before him left him breathless. He *had* to be dreaming!

"The last time we were together, you asked me an important question. I couldn't give you an answer then, but I'm prepared to give you one now. But maybe too much time has passed and you'd like to unask it."

He could hardly breathe. "Remind me of the question."

"You asked me to be your wife." The tremor in her voice made its way to his heart.

"I remember. But you had an irreconcilable conflict that prevented you from answering."

Her eyes filled with tears. "Since then I've *un*-conflicted it."

His breath caught in his lungs. "How was that possible?"

"Two days ago I flew to Rome and had the conversation with Dea we've needed to have since she visited me in Catania. It was the heart-to-heart kind that immersed two sisters in tears. It was a time of love and forgiveness for all past hurts and misunderstandings. In the end she told me something I needed desperately to hear. So do you.

"She said, 'I wanted Rini Montanari to want me, so I made a play for him and kissed him good-night right on the mouth. He didn't bite.'"

Rini's head reared. "She admitted that to you?"

"Oh, yes. There's more. She said she invited you to dinner but you turned her down flat."

He shook his head. "I don't believe what I'm hearing."

"I do. That's because you're an honorable

man, my darling. Not only for turning her down because you didn't have those kinds of feelings for her, but for keeping that secret to yourself in order not to hurt her or me. She thinks I'm the luckiest woman alive. I am! She said to tell you that she welcomes you to the Caracciolo family with open arms. That's a good thing because I plan to be your wife. I can't live without you!"

She ran into his arms, almost knocking him over while she covered his face and mouth with kisses. "*Ti amo*, Rini. *Ti amo*."

"Hey, bro?"

Rini's eyes swerved to the door. Carlo had just walked in on them, but he came to an abrupt standstill and a huge smile broke out on his face. "Well, look what my *fratello* snagged on his last fishing trip! I wouldn't have missed this for the world. Looks like Guido's the only living bachelor left in Naples. I'll make sure you're not disturbed."

He closed the door. By now Rini had sat down in his chair with Alessandra in his lap.

They kissed long and hard until he started to believe this was really happening. She looked and smelled divine.

"How soon can we get married, *bellissima*?"

"Whenever you want. I think the chapel in the castle would be the perfect place. Dea and I had a chapel in our play castle. We always planned elaborate weddings with our dolls. We even had a doll priest. Did you know Queen Joanna married one of her husbands there?"

Rini hugged her hard. "I can't think of a place more fitting for you."

"And you, because you're my prince. We'll invite all our friends and family. We have room for everyone. The cook will plan a wedding feast with all the fish you can eat." He started chuckling. "Dea will help me find the perfect wedding dress and Fulvia will help Mamma do everything else. We'll ask your sister to bring her babies and we'll dress them up like little princes. Alfredo will walk around excited because there's going to be food. And Papà will play the host with a twinkle in his eye."

By now his chuckling had turned to deep laughter. "There's one thing *I* want to do. Plan the honeymoon," he whispered against the side of her neck.

"I was hoping you'd say that. Can we leave now and go somewhere private where I can kiss you as long and wickedly as I want?"

"What a ridiculous question to ask the man who's headlong in love with the most gorgeous woman alive."

"I hope you'll always feel that way."

It took them a while to stop kissing long enough to make it to the roof. Rini told his pilot to fly them to Positano. "We're getting married, Lucca."

He grinned. "Tonight?"

"Don't I wish. It'll be soon."

With a background of Vesuvius, the helicopter rose into the evening sky. Rini was so full of emotion, he couldn't talk. While they were in the air, he pulled a ring out of his breast pocket. He'd bought it a month ago and had been carrying it around, keeping it close to him like a talisman.

"Give me your left hand, *adorata*."

Her whole countenance beamed as she did his bidding. He slid the ring on her finger. "It's fabulous, Rini!" She held it up close to inspect it. "The diamond and setting—this is like the one on Queen Joanna's hand in the foyer of the castle!"

"The foyer was the place I fell in love with you. She's the reason you and I met. In a way I owe her my life. I'm glad you noticed."

Her beautiful eyes rounded. "You silly man. How could I not notice? Just wait till you see the ring I have planned for you."

Joy was a new emotion for him. So new, he clung to her hand, unable to find words.

CHAPTER NINE

ALESSANDRA STOOD OUTSIDE the closed chapel doors with her father, where they could hear the organ playing. After waiting a month for her wedding day, she was so anxious to be Rini's wife, she'd started to feel feverish in anticipation.

"Papà? Why are we waiting?" Everyone was inside including her husband-to-be, whom she knew was equally impatient to be married at this point.

Her distinguished-looking father, outfitted in wedding finery and a blue sash befitting the Count of Caracciolo, turned to her with a gleam in his eyes. "Your aunt has worked her magic."

"What do you mean?"

"As you are a princess of the Houses of Taranto

and Caraciolla, the Archbishop of Taranto is going to preside. We're giving him time to enter the nave through the side entrance."

A quiet gasp escaped her. "Rini's not going to believe it."

"He's going to have to get used to a lot of surprises being married to my darling *piccola.*"

She smiled at him. "You're loving this, aren't you?"

He leaned over and kissed her forehead. "Almost as much as you. After all the weddings performed in your playhouse castle, you're going to be the star in your very own. You look like an angel in all that white fluff and lace."

"Dea found it for me."

"Of course. That explains the long train."

"It's spectacular."

"So are you. I see your mother gave you her tiara to wear."

"Something old and borrowed. Papà? Do you like Rini? I mean really like him?"

"I think he's an exceptional man who has met his match in you."

While they stood there, Dea came around the corner toward them. She looked a vision in pale lavender carrying two bouquets. She handed the one made of white roses to Alessandra. "I outdid myself when I picked out this wedding dress for you."

"I love it. I love you."

"Do you know where you're going on your honeymoon yet?"

"Rini's lips are sealed."

"Lucky you." Dea kissed her. "It's time."

The doors suddenly opened and Dea took her place behind Alessandra and her father. Together they entered the ornate chapel with its stained glass windows, where a lot of history had been made. Every single person she loved was assembled. The archbishop added a solemnity to the occasion in his ceremonial robes. But she only had eyes for the tall, dark-haired man turned out in dove-gray wedding clothes standing near the altar.

The dazzling white of his dress shirt set off his olive skin coloring to perfection. He was her prince in every sense of the word. She prayed her heart wouldn't give out before she reached his side. His dark eyes seemed to leap to hers as she reached his side. While the archbishop addressed the congregation, Rini didn't remove his gaze from her.

"Surely heaven is shining down on these two people this day while they are joined together in the most holy ordinance of the church," the archbishop began.

Rini's hand held hers. He rubbed his thumb over her palm and wrist. She was trying to concentrate on the sacredness of the occasion, but his touch sent fire through her entire body. By the time they came to exchanging vows, he'd reduced her to a weakened state. Thank heaven the words were finally pronounced.

"I now pronounce you, Rinieri di Brazzano

Montanari, and you, Alessandra Taranto Caracciolo, man and wife in front of God and this congregation. What God has joined together, let no man put asunder."

Her clear conscience over Dea had freed her from bondage. They both kissed with restrained passion, forcing themselves to hold back. But she was bursting inside with love for him. When she turned to face her family, her joy was so great she could hardly contain it.

"It won't be long now," Rini whispered in an aside. He squeezed her hand as he led them down the aisle and out the doors to the great dining hall that had once seen the courtiers of kings and queens. He reached around her waist and pressed her against his hip while they greeted their parents and guests. She saw her father hand something to Rini before they took their places at the head table.

Guido and his parents sat together before he took over the emcee job. "One good thing about this marriage. Alessandra has taken him off the market. Now *I'm* the most famous bachelor of Naples." He ended with a wonderful trail of anecdotes about Rini that had people bursting with laughter.

Dea took her turn. "Alessandra and I were joined at the hip in the womb. It feels strange to be on my own at last, but I couldn't be happier for her." She shared more nuggets of personal moments with Alessandra to delight their audience. Alessandra turned beet-red.

One by one, the members of both families paid tribute. Valentina brought tears to everyone's eyes in her tribute to Rini, who'd been so wonderful to her after their mother had died. Carlo reminisced over his own touching memories of Rini when their mother was alive.

There were more speeches, but she could tell Rini was restless. In a move that appeared to surprise him, she rose to her feet with some difficulty considering the length of her train. "Rini and I want to thank everyone for making our wedding day unforgettable. Zia Fulvia? What would we do without you? In fact, what would we do without our marvelous staff, my darling Liona and her cat Alfredo and the families we cherish."

Rini got to his feet. "I couldn't have said it better, but I hope you'll understand that we need to leave."

"Sure you do," Guido quipped loud enough for everyone to hear. Dea laughed at his remark. Alessandra hid her head against Rini's shoulder as they left the hall on a run. He led her through the hallway to the foyer. They raced out the doors to the Land Rover. He stuffed her inside and ran around to drive them to the helipad.

Their pilot was all smiles as he helped her on board. Once they were strapped in, they took off with Rini seated in the copilot's seat. "*Complimenti*, Signora Montanari."

"*Grazie*, Lucca. My husband won't tell me where we're going."

"We'll be there soon, *bellissima*."

"It was a beautiful wedding, don't you think?"

"Yes, but I thought it would never be over."

"Mamma said the wedding is for the bride. She was right."

The pilot flew east to the Adriatic, then dropped to a luxury yacht making its way through the water. Her eyes darted to Rini's in question.

"Guido's parents insisted on providing their yacht for our honeymoon. We can stop anywhere we want and scuba dive in Croatian waters. There are caves you'll love to explore."

"It sounds wonderful, but as you once told me, I don't care where we go as long as we're together."

Lucca set them down on the yacht's helipad with remarkable expertise. Rini jumped out and reached for her, carrying her across the deck to a stairway with the master bedroom on the next level down. She could see everything had been prepared for them ahead of time. Flowers overflowed the living area of the suite, creating a heavenly perfume.

"At last." The way he was looking at her caused her limbs to quiver. He wrapped his arms around her and undid the buttons of her wedding dress, while he gave her a husband's kiss that never ended.

Somehow they gravitated to the bedroom, leaving a trail of wedding clothes and a tiara. The covers had been turned down. He followed her on to the mattress, burying his face in her throat. "Alessandra, I can't believe you're my wife. I've been lonely for you for years."

"You don't know the half of it. I love you so terribly. Make love to me, darling, and never ever stop," she murmured feverishly until they were devouring each other and conversation ceased.

For the rest of the night they communicated with their bodies, trying to show each other how they felt in ways that words couldn't. Rini took her to another world, where she felt transformed. When morning came she couldn't bear for the night to be over. Even though he'd finally fallen asleep, she started kissing him again to wake him up. His eyes opened.

"You've married a wanton. Forgive me."

In a surprise move he rolled her over so he was looking down at her. "I wouldn't have you any other way. You're perfect." Another long, deep kiss ensued.

"But was it...good for you?"

He moaned. "What a question to ask me? Can't you tell what you've done? I'll never want to go to work again."

"I don't know if I'll be able to let you go."

"Then our problem is solved. *Buongiorno, moglie mia.* Welcome to my world."

She pressed another avid kiss to his compelling mouth. "We're not dreaming this, are we? This is real. You really are my husband."

"You'd better believe it, but in case you're in any doubt, let me prove it."

To her joy he proved it over and over. Except for taking the time to eat, she drowned in her husband's love. They didn't surface for three days.

At the end of that time they planned to go up on deck. But before they left their room, Alessandra rushed around in her robe to pick up their wedding attire still all over the room. It would be too embarrassing for any of the ship's staff to see the hurry they'd been in after arriving in the helicopter after the ceremony.

"Darling? I found this in the pocket of your suit." He'd just come out of the bathroom with a towel hitched around his hips. She handed him an envelope.

"Your father slipped this to me at the castle."

"I wondered what it was."

Rini opened it and pulled out a letter.

"What does it say?

"'Alessandra's mother and I wanted to give you a wedding present, but it's for selfish reasons on our part. If you want to drill on our land, you have our permission. That way we know we'll see you part of the time when you have to be at the castle to supervise every-thing.'"

He looked shocked. Alessandra slid her arms up his chest and around his neck. "Now you know how much they love and trust you."

"I never expected this."

"That's one of the reasons why they did it. But my guess is, Fulvia helped Mother see that your vision can help our country."

"Is that what you think, too? Your opinion is the one that matters to me."

"You know I do. Otherwise I would never have taken you to see my aunt."

"We can thank providence you did. She proved to be the catalyst that helped you and your sister put away your demons."

She nodded. "One problem solved and one to go."

He kissed her with almost primitive desire. "We don't have another one."

"You're almost thirty-three and not getting any younger. Neither am I. If we're going to adopt children, we need to do something about it soon. These things can take time."

His brow dipped. "Are you desperate for a child already? Or tired of me already?"

"Rini... I'm not going to dignify either of those questions with a response. I'm simply looking ahead to our future. When I saw you playing with Ric and Vito a couple of days ago, I could picture you playing with our own children.

"I'm not saying we're ready now. Maybe the day will come when you'll want to consult one of the attorneys who work for you and we'll make an application to begin the process. But if it upsets you, I promise I'll never bring it up again."

He let out a ragged sigh and crushed her in his arms. "I'm sorry I got so defensive. It's different when you know you can't have your own baby. I don't know if I could be a good father."

"No one knows if they're going to be able to

handle it. I bet if you ask Carlo, he'll tell you he was nervous before their daughter was born."

"But he knew it was his."

"But he didn't see the baby until she was born. If we adopt, we won't see the baby until it's born. What difference will it make?"

He smiled. "You're right. It won't."

"Come on. Let's go on deck and soak up a little sun."

"I have a better idea. How would you like to fly to Montenegro for dinner? We've been away from the ship for three days. Wear that gorgeous outfit you showed up in at my office."

"You liked that one? I'll start getting ready right now."

"I like you in anything when you have to wear clothes, but if I had my way..."

"That works for me where you're concerned too." She giggled and ran into the bathroom, but he caught up to her before she could lock the door.

EPILOGUE

Eight months later

RINI WAS AT the drilling site when his cell rang. Hopefully it was Alessandra telling him she was back at the castle after her visit to her editor in Rome. Her book on Queen Joanna would be coming out shortly and the publisher wanted to set up some book signings.

But when he checked the caller ID, he saw that it was Maso Vanni, the attorney who'd helped him and Alessandra make application for adoption. The unmarried mother from Naples who'd been the right match for them was expecting her baby in a month. Rini hoped everything was all right. The last thing he wanted was to give his wife bad news.

He clicked on. "Maso? What's going on?"

"Lauretta Conti is in labor."

"What?"

"The doctor is trying to slow things down, but my advice is for you and your wife to get to the hospital as soon as you can."

"We'll be there!" He rang off and phoned Alessandra, but her voice mail was on. He left her the message that he was on his way to the hospital in Naples because Lauretta Conti might be having her baby in the next little while.

After leaving instructions with the crew, he drove to Metaponto for his helicopter flight to the hospital in Naples. There was no time to shower or change out of his khaki work clothes. En route he tried several times to reach Alessandra. "Please answer as soon as you can, *cara.*"

Once at the hospital he was shown to Lauretta's private room. The doctor said they couldn't stop the baby from coming. "My patient needs a Caesarean. You're about to become a father."

Rini had never felt so helpless in his life.

"The nurse will show you where to scrub."

The situation was surreal as he washed and put on a gown. He was given a mask and gloves. Before long he returned to the room and stood by the head of the bed. He and Alessandra had met with Lauretta several times in preparation for the baby's arrival. Where was his wife?

Suddenly things began to happen. The anesthesiologist administered a spinal and a team came in while the doctor performed surgery. Everyone seemed so calm. When he heard a gurgling sound, a thrill shot through him. A second later the newborn cry of the baby filled the room.

The pediatrician took over and Rini was told to follow him to the room next door. "I understand you're going to be the father of this baby."

"Yes." But fear held him in its grip.

"Where's your wife?"

"She's on her way." She would be when she got the message.

"He's strong for a preemie. Six pounds, twenty-one inches long. Seems to be breathing on his own. As soon as we clean him up, you can hold him."

The baby had a dusting of dark hair. Rini watched in fascination as the doctor checked him out. One of the nurses came in and put the baby in a little shirt and diaper, then wrapped him in a receiving blanket.

"Sit down, *signore*, so you can hold your son."

Nothing had seemed real until she placed the baby in Rini's arms and he was able to look at him. The sight of the beautiful boy caused his heart to melt. He didn't make a peep. Rini couldn't tell the color of his eyes yet. His little mouth made an *O*.

"You've got a cute *bambino* there," the nurse said. "Don't be afraid of him. He won't break. I'll get a bottle ready for him."

Taking her advice, he put the baby on his shoulder and patted his back. The warmth of his tiny body was a revelation. Emotion swamped him as he realized this baby would look to him forever as his father. Rini removed the mask and kissed his little head, wanting to be all things to him. A longing to protect him and give him everything possible filled his soul.

"Here you go." The nurse handed him the bottle. "He'll be hungry soon. Tease his mouth with the nipple and he'll start to suck."

He followed her advice. Like magic the baby responded and started to drink with gusto. "Hey, you like this, don't you? I like food, too. I'm a big eater. Always have been."

"Like father, like son." His wife's voice.

He turned his head. "Alessandra... How long have you been standing there?"

"Long enough to watch you bond with him. I knew it would happen."

Tears filled his eyes. "It did. I was terrified when I got here, but when the nurse put him in my arms..."

She smiled down at both of them. "Fatherhood took over."

"You need to hold him."

"I will in a minute. It's enough to watch the two of you. What did the pediatrician say?"

"He seems fine and his lungs are functioning even though he came early."

"We're so blessed." Her eyes glistened with moisture. "Can you believe we're parents now? I'm a new mom and didn't even have to go through labor."

"You're the most gorgeous mother in the world."

"And you're already a natural father. I can tell he's so happy to be there with you. He has almost finished his bottle."

She put her arms around his shoulders and stared down at the baby with her cheek against Rini's. "We're going to learn how to do this minute by minute. I love you for being willing to adopt. I know it wasn't an easy decision to make."

Rini was close to being overcome by his deepest feelings. "I never dreamed I would see this day."

"I know. It's a surprise since you're a true man of vision."

He cleared his throat. "I don't think you have any idea how much I love you for marrying me when you knew I couldn't give you a baby."

"But you *have* given me one, darling. He's in your arms and you're both in mine. What more could a woman ask for in this life?"

* * * * *

MILLS & BOON®
Large Print – September 2016

Morelli's Mistress
Anne Mather

A Tycoon to Be Reckoned With
Julia James

Billionaire Without a Past
Carol Marinelli

The Shock Cassano Baby
Andie Brock

The Most Scandalous Ravensdale
Melanie Milburne

The Sheikh's Last Mistress
Rachael Thomas

Claiming the Royal Innocent
Jennifer Hayward

The Billionaire Who Saw Her Beauty
Rebecca Winters

In the Boss's Castle
Jessica Gilmore

One Week with the French Tycoon
Christy McKellen

Rafael's Contract Bride
Nina Milne

MILLS & BOON®
Large Print – October 2016

Wallflower, Widow...Wife!
Ann Lethbridge

Bought for the Greek's Revenge
Lynne Graham

An Heir to Make a Marriage
Abby Green

The Greek's Nine-Month Redemption
Maisey Yates

Expecting a Royal Scandal
Caitlin Crews

Return of the Untamed Billionaire
Carol Marinelli

Signed Over to Santino
Maya Blake

Wedded, Bedded, Betrayed
Michelle Smart

The Greek's Nine-Month Surprise
Jennifer Faye

A Baby to Save Their Marriage
Scarlet Wilson

Stranded with Her Rescuer
Nikki Logan

Expecting the Fellani Heir
Lucy Gordon